WRITERS REPUBLIC

Drowning
in You

CAROLINE JUSTICE

WRITERS REPUBLIC L.L.C.
515 Summit Ave. Unit R1
Union City, NJ 07087, USA

Website: *www.writersrepublic.com*
Hotline: *1-877-656-6838*
Email: *info@writersrepublic.com*

Ordering Information:
Quantity sales. Special discounts are available on quantity purchases by corporations, associations, and others. For details, contact the publisher at the address above.

Library of Congress Control Number:		2021937074
ISBN-13:	978-1-63728-414-8	[Paperback Edition]
	978-1-63728-415-5	[Digital Edition]

Rev. date: 04/05/2021

Dedicated to my fiancé, my forever love, the one who has supported me through writing this book the most. He has always been willing to put my dreams first whether it's moving across the country or with the reassuring words of "I'm proud of you" and "You've got this." Thank you for always being there for me and being my greatest love story.

1

OLIVER

I walked down the halls of NYU in a blur, passing people that I didn't care about; nodding to those that were lucky enough to catch my attention, not many people did. I like to think that I am a social person but only with those that in my mind mattered. I have a lot of friends and those are the people I talk to. If you aren't one of those people then sorry, apply again next year. I'm on the swim team and I know girls watch me, why wouldn't they? I have great abs and a nice ass if I do say so myself. It doesn't matter to me though. Okay, so there is one person that I wouldn't mind getting closer to.

My thoughts were interrupted as a kid bumped into me. I looked down to see a kid with jet black hair, a black Green Day t-shirt, and black skinny jeans on. His head was looking down as he mumbled his apology and rushed off. I didn't have to see his face to know who he was, I'd been watching him. I had first noticed him one day when I got out of the pool and he was sitting up in the bleachers reading a book and listening to music. I hadn't thought that much about him until the next day when I saw him sitting outside the cafeteria, alone. He didn't exactly look lonely, more like he was content. The only thing that stopped me from thinking he was happy sitting alone was when he caught me staring, and when our eyes locked and he looked back at me with those dark chocolate brown eyes I could see so many years of sadness in them. Almost as if he wasn't content with the solitude but had just gotten used to it. Those eyes are what made me watch him, even though I never noticed other people. From that day on I noticed him everywhere; in the halls, walking home, in the cafeteria, the pool, I would walk by classrooms, and out of all of the people sitting inside I would notice him sitting in the furthest corner away from everybody. His presence was so understated that it was hard not to notice him. Everyone else tried so hard to be noticed and he tried so little. But those eyes of his are what made me want to notice him. I mean hey, it isn't like I just stalked the guy and never said anything. I tried to talk to him once. Just once. I would've been better off not saying anything because it was as if I hadn't in the first place. As in, I made absolutely no impression on him.

What happened was this:

I was going to sit with my group of friends at lunch but then I noticed him sitting in his usual spot outside. I couldn't help it, I left my friends and went outside. I walked up to his table and sat my tray down. I thought maybe he would enjoy the company since he always sat alone. Boy was I wrong.

"Someone is sitting there." He said in a bored tone of voice not even looking up.

"Just here?" I asked questioningly. I was a little confused, no one ever sat with this kid.

"No, all of the seats are taken." He said without looking up again.

"Are you sure? 'Cause I've noticed every day, no one ever sits with you." He seemed to flinch at my words. I felt as if that was a little mean but hey I was trying to be nice to this kid and he was icing me out. I'm supposed to be the one that doesn't care about those that are outside my bubble, that was my thing.

"Well then maybe I just don't want to sit with you." He said with venom in his tone and he set his book down angrily and looked up. I could tell by his expression that he was surprised that it was me. I never talked to outsiders. But he quickly regained his composure and his face lost all emotion again.

"Aww, you wound me," I said with a mock expression of pain and my hands over my heart as if he had shot me. What can I say? I'm a sarcastic guy.

"Whatever, I don't care." He said going back to his book.

I took that as an invitation to sit and quickly began eating my food. This kid didn't care much about anything, did he?

We sat there in silence for what felt like ages. I decided to try my hand at a conversation.

"So, my name's Oliver by the way," I said in between bites of my quesadilla.

"Whatever." He said his face is still buried in his book.

"And your name is . . . ?" I asked, prompting the conversation on.

He shut his book aggressively and looked up at me and said, "Why do you care?"

"Just trying to diffuse the tension."

"Well don't. I don't wanna talk to you right now. Why do you think I sit by myself?"

"Just thought you were like me," I said shrugging.

This seemed to take him off guard as if he wasn't expecting him and I could have anything in common.

"What do you mean?" He asked, his face looking less aggressive as his features relaxed. Now that I was looking at his face I could tell he wasn't that bad looking. I mean he just had that kind of sinister aura, like he'd seen things that would make others cry.

3

"I mean, like, you don't mix well with other people. You don't care. Almost like you're comfortable away from everyone else." I said, my head getting a little fuzzy. I had never explained to others why I didn't want them around, I just avoided them and made them think I just didn't like them.

Then he said something in a sort of mumble and I said, "What?"

"I said, 'My name is Raven.'"

After that, he never talked to me again, but at least I knew his name now.

2

RAVEN

I can't believe I just ran into him. I hadn't even talked to him since that day he sat next to me at my usual lunch table. I mean I'm not complaining, I liked being alone. Oh, who was I kidding? I hated it! It wasn't like I wanted to be alone, I just ended up that way. No one talked to me because they thought I was weird and creepy. I mean I get it, I kind of give off that vibe. But that doesn't mean I like to be alone, but I am comfortable alone. I don't know how to explain it. It's almost like when I am around other people I feel pressured to act happy even when I'm not. I don't like that, and I really don't know what happiness feels like anymore, I haven't felt that in years, so I find it hard to pretend. It's almost as if a teacher tells you to write an essay about something that you don't understand and have never heard of. It's hard and even if you finish it everyone knows you just bullshitted your way through it and end up making a fool out of yourself. That's why I don't spend time around other people, to avoid the bullshit. If I don't interact then I don't have to pretend.

I look over my shoulder to see if he is still there, he is. He stopped in the hallway after I ran into him and I think he's looking for me. I don't think he'll notice me, no one ever really does. I just blend into the shadows. They might glance at me once in a while but they never truly see me. I watch Oliver for another second before I continue walking down the hallway toward my mythology course. I don't know what it is about her class but it is always the best part of my day, other than when I'm sitting in the hallway up against the wall and I notice Oliver watching me. He was the only one that actually saw me when I normally was invisible.

I sat in my usual spot in the back of the classroom and put my headphones on and switched to some Red Jumpsuit Apparatus. I love this band, their music is always exactly what I need. I space out for a while until I notice movement at the door. Someone was standing in front of the window in the door watching me, it was Oliver. When our eyes met he gave me a smirk and a small wave and then continued walking down the hallway. How often does he watch me like that?

I stared down at my desk and thought of every time I had noticed him watching me. There were a lot. I'd have to ask him about that one day.

OLIVER

As I was walking down the hall I saw him through the window. I stopped and watched him sitting in his usual place as his head nodded to the music he was listening to. His head stopped nodding and he slowly turned his head to meet my gaze. I smirked at him and gave him a small nod and then I started walking down the hallway again. There was just something in those deep brown eyes that made me want to get closer to him. I just loved those eyes.

When I got back to my class all I could do was think of Raven, his eyes, the way he spaces out, the way he hides behind his black bangs. I love how he walked confidently but still managed to keep his head low, almost as if he was trying to distance himself from everyone. Right then I promised myself that I was going to get closer to Raven, starting with me meeting up with him after class.

RAVEN

I was shaken out of my daydreams by the sound of the bell signaling the end of class. I gathered up all of my stuff and started walking for the door. As I exited my path was instantly blocked by Oliver. I almost ran into him but I stopped just in time. I mumbled my apology and tried to walk around him but he swung his arm around my shoulders and started walking with me.

"What are you doing?" I asked, thoroughly confused. No one ever walked with me let alone in this position. As we walked people glanced at us strangely, the attention made me anxious. I tried to shrug off his arm but he wasn't having it, he gripped his hand to my shoulder.

"So what do you have planned for today after school, Raven?" Oliver asked nonchalantly.

I blushed slightly at the personal question and said, "I dunno. I'll probably just go home and watch a movie."

"That sounds fun! Why don't I meet you after school and then we can go over to my place and watch a movie instead?" He asked happily. Oliver is weird. No one ever wants to spend time with me, let alone invite me over to their house.

"I guess? Where do you wanna meet up?" I asked, slightly confused. Why is he acting like this? Does he really want to spend time with me? I don't really know what to do in this sort of situation. I'm not really equipped to deal with people. I really don't wanna go. I don't like being around people for long periods of time. Trust me, if I could get away with not coming to school at all then I wouldn't be in this situation right now. Maybe I didn't really have to go. Maybe I could just tell him I would and then just not show up at the meeting point. I could just ditch him.

Oliver walked with me to my next class and then smiled and waved at me as I disappeared through the doorway. Throughout my class, I couldn't help but think about Oliver. I remembered how we first met and how he told me that he thought we were alike. How he just didn't care enough to mix with other people. I was the exact opposite, although he would probably never guess it. It wasn't that I didn't care enough, it was that I cared too much. I cared about who I was when I was around other people. I wasn't myself, no one liked the real me. But maybe he might like the real me. I thought to myself. I shook the thought from my mind. I don't really know anything about Oliver, and he doesn't really know anything about me. Anything that I might think I know about him is just built on either what he wants people to know about him or gossip.

3

OLIVER

I waited there for fifteen minutes. He obviously stood me up. I mean I get it, he doesn't like people. Maybe I was just a little too aggressive, baby steps Miller. I turned to leave when I heard someone approach from behind me. I stopped and turned around, there was Raven.

"Took you long enough." I said sarcastically. Wait, did he just blush? Had to have been my imagination. Weird, I kind of want him to blush.

"I wanted to see how long you would wait for me." He said with his head bowed but I could see him looking at me with those intriguing brown eyes through his bangs. His comment made something stir within me, a feeling I'm not exactly familiar with.

"So you were testing me?" I asked and he flinched at my question. I'm not sure how I felt about that. Was I just happy he showed up? Angry that he strung me along for so long? No, it was that feeling, the one I can't quite place.

"Did I pass?" I asked. I don't get the best grades in school but when it came to being around Raven I wanted to pass. I wanted to get the best grade possible. I wanted him to feel happy around me and to let me get close to him.

We started walking towards my car and I opened the door for him.

Raven blushed slightly when I opened it and gestured for him to get inside. That's when I understood what he was thinking, this kind of seemed like a date. I blushed a little too and explained, "Sorry, there is a trick to opening it. You have to wiggle the handle." The excuse sounded lame even to me but I don't want him to think this is a date. Or did I? Is this a date? Do I want it to be? Does he wish this were a date?

RAVEN

The ride to Oliver's house felt like it took eons rather than minutes. I couldn't help but steal glances at him as he drove. Once he caught me looking and asked me what was wrong. I couldn't tell him what I was thinking though. It would mess everything up. I couldn't help but think how Oliver's smell filled the air, it was almost intoxicating. I loved how the sun shined through the windshield and caused his eyes to sparkle. The intense blue made me feel like I was drowning, the gold flecks like sun rays on the ocean waves, and a splash of seafoam green. They seemed to go on forever. His hair is jet black. Messy, kind of like he just rolled out of bed. I loved the way his hair brushed across his forehead and framed his face just so. Made me think about just how attractive Oliver really was. There wasn't anything about him that wasn't mesmerizing. His looks, his smile, his personality, the way he could say anything and make all the blood in my body rush to my face, and other places.

I shifted in my seat as I thought about that time I saw him at the pool. The way his abs glistened and the water trickled down his stomach toward the one place I wanted to discover most. I blushed again at my thoughts. I had to stop thinking like this otherwise I was going to find myself in a very awkward situation if he looked over. But the image of him in his bathing suit made me shiver with want. It was going to be a long night if I kept this up. But when you're sitting next to someone as sexy as Oliver, it's hard to keep your thoughts pure.

I sigh thinking about everything I would love to do to Oliver, to have done to me. There were endless possibilities. What would I do just to run my fingers through his hair? To tell him how I've always wanted to be this close.

OLIVER

I can tell he's watching me, I had already caught him once.

Once I looked over at him and he had the strangest look on his face, almost as if he was having a war inside his head. The look of inner turmoil was so prominent I wished I could read his mind. Maybe then I'd be able to understand him better.

Once I swear I heard him sigh, but it wasn't like a bored sigh or an exasperated one. It almost sounded like longing. Now I really wanted to read his mind, to find out who he was thinking about. Is it bad that I want it to be me? The thought of him sighing like that while thinking about me brings a smile to my face. I see him shift in his seat out of the corner of my eye and that makes me curious. Is he uncomfortable?

I look over at him once again and ask, "What are you thinking about?" A feeling of triumph rises from within me as the blood rushes to his pale cheeks and paints them red. I'm pretty sure he was thinking about me if I made him blush when he thought about it. The thought of that causes my heart to leap within my chest. Maybe he does like me. I think to myself.

With every turn I take I can't seem to keep my focus on the road, it keeps wandering to the person sitting in my passenger seat. I keep seeing him in my mind. I visualized kissing his lips. They looked so soft I was tempted to stop the car and kiss him right now just to find out, but I'm not so sure that Raven would be okay with that.

I visualized us back at my place, him laying on the couch with me on top of him kissing him with so much passion and ferocity that it shocked me. I needed to stop thinking about this otherwise I was gonna get hard and scare him away. But then again I could see me slipping my hand up his shirt and pinching his nipple. The sound of his moan echoing in my ears. God, I wonder what his moan sounds like. I want to know what it tastes like to explore every part of him, his mouth, his nipples, his neck, his thighs. God what about his cock, what would it taste like to have that inside my mouth, the feeling of his come dripping down my throat?

I shook my head to clear the lustful mist from my mind as I focused on my driving. That didn't last long. I want to know all of it. I had to know. What would it feel like to slam my rock hard cock into his soft, white ass? God, I hope I get the chance to find out.

All these new emotions were foreign but not unwelcome. I'm not used to thinking about guys in that way. Honestly, this would be the first time. I've only ever dated girls up to this point, but I wouldn't even count those as being experiences to cement my sexuality. I'd only gone that far with one girl and even though it was great and I'd definitely be with a female again I knew that bisexuality was a thing. I could definitely be bi. Especially knowing first hand my attraction to Raven.

RAVEN

We couldn't get to his house soon enough.

I was starting to imagine what it would feel like to run my tongue down his abs. I imagined sliding his cock between my lips, sucking on him, and playing with his balls until he released his load into my mouth. I would lick my lips to get every last drop of him. These thoughts sent a chill down my spine. STOP! I mentally screamed at myself. But then the image of Oliver's face buried between my ass cheeks as he licked and fingered my hole came into my mind. Just the thought of it made me want to moan.

When the car stopped I got out of the car as fast as possible and tried to adjust myself to where Oliver wouldn't notice the obvious bulge in my, now too tight, skinny jeans. As we walked inside I noticed how Oliver was walking differently. Is it possible he noticed my hard-on? Oh god I hope not, that would be mortifying.

We got inside and Oliver indicated that he was going to go to the bathroom real fast but to make myself comfortable on the couch and to pick out a movie I wanted to watch. I took this time to try and cool off. I mean what the hell?! Why was I getting so worked up over Oliver? Maybe it's his ass? I asked myself. Then mentally slapped myself. You're supposed to be calming down not getting worked up! Maybe it was that hard-on he was sporting as he awkwardly walked into the bathroom? Oh my God shut up! I scream at myself.

4

OLIVER

I close the door to the bathroom calmly and begin fumbling with my buckle.

'I can't believe I'm doing this.' I think to myself as I pull my hard cock into my hand and start jerking it quickly. All I can think about is Raven; his full lips and how they would feel wrapped around my rock hard erection, me pounding into his tight ass as he cried out and moaned. The thoughts swirling around in my head surged me toward the finish as my imagination went wild. I exploded into my hand and a feeling of shame enveloped me. What would Raven think if he knew what I was doing here? Would he be disgusted by the thought of me using him in my fantasies? Would he shudder at my touch and run away?

I clean myself up and gather my thoughts. I need to calm down. The last thing I want is to scare him away. I take a deep breath and open the door.

RAVEN

When Oliver came back he looked a lot better than he had before. He wasn't walking funny, his complexion was almost glowing, and he seemed more eager. As he bent down to insert the disk into the DVD player I couldn't help but stare at that sexy swimmer's ass of his. I couldn't help that he made me think of sinful thoughts.

I scolded myself silently and sat down on the couch. I kicked my shoes off and swung my feet up next to me hoping that this would encourage him to sit further away. It did not. Oliver sat next to me with his jean-clad thigh touching my feet just enough to send pulses of electricity through my whole body.

OLIVER

As we watched the movie I couldn't concentrate. Every time I looked at the screen I glanced at Raven, then I thought about the sexy version of him in my daydreams and what I'd like to do to him right on this couch. Just sitting on the couch from my daydreams gave me a slight chub. I grabbed the blanket that was folded over the back of the couch and draped it over my crotch and legs. The last thing I needed was for him to see the ever-growing bulge in my pants.

I slightly shifted closer to Raven, he didn't pull away. Could I try a little closer? I risked it. I inched a little closer and he lowered his feet from the couch, subconsciously making more room for me. I scooted closer again this time making our shoulders touch ever so slightly. Raven's head dipped slightly as he started to drift and then leaned his head on my shoulder. This made me smile. I slowly reached my arm up and rested it on the back of the couch careful not to touch him so that he would continue to sleep. He looked up at me sleepily and gave me a small smile before falling back asleep.

I slowly eased my arm onto his shoulders. I was surprised. You couldn't tell from the look of him but he had a little muscle. Not enough to bulk but I could tell he was lean. I liked that. Raven stirred slightly, then relaxed and curled himself into the space between my arm and chest. I wrapped my arm around his shoulders, he nuzzled against me. I smiled slightly, everything was going pretty well.

When the movie ended Raven rose from my chest slightly and got up to leave when he noticed the movie had ended during his slumber. I tightened my grip around his shoulders. I didn't want him to leave. I could stay forever with him sleeping on my chest. Just listening to his sighs and quiet breathing.

13

"Where are you going?" I asked with disappointment littering my tone. I didn't want him to leave yet. I had just gotten him to relax around me.

"Home?" He said, confused. Then he noticed the look on my face and said, "Or not?"

That made me smile. He eased back against me and I kissed his hair gently. He smelled like cinnamon; it made me want to be with him even longer, get even closer to him.

RAVEN

We were cuddling on the couch and then Oliver kissed the top of my head. Everything he did made me want to jump him. I looked up at him and smiled. I don't think I'll ever fully understand this sexy being sitting next to me.

He leaned his head slightly down towards me and then stopped an inch or two away from my face. His eyes flickered in between my eyes and my lips. Did he want to kiss me? I threw caution to the wind and closed the remaining distance between us. Our lips crashed together and their connection sent a bolt of electricity through my body, I shivered at the sensation. Our lips moved together in a sort of kissing tango, every time I wanted more he could tell. He was a good kisser, not too wet and not too much tongue. I wanted more of him. Oliver started to push against me and I leaned backward, lying down completely on the couch. He climbed on top of me and straddled me. He explored my mouth and I marveled at the taste of him. I had been wondering what he would taste like since the first day I saw him. His lips were so soft and warm, the way they moved expertly against mine. Oliver nibbled on my bottom lip and then moved his attention to my jawline. He grazed my earlobe and then left a hickey on my collarbone. He bit at the skin where my neck and shoulders connected and I let out an involuntary moan. He was good at this. My arms wrapped around him and I gripped at the shirt on his back.

"Oliver," I moaned. "Too many clothes."

I felt a chuckle vibrate against my skin and he quickly removed his shirt revealing those abs that I've longed to run my tongue over. Then he grabbed hold of my shirt and pulled it over my head. He leaned down and sucked one nipple into his mouth and teased it. His teeth bit at it gently and his tongue rolled it in his mouth. As he did this a strangled moan escapes my mouth.

"Mmmmmmm." I moan loudly.

He reached up and pinched my other nipple as he continued his oral inspection of the other. Waves of pleasure coursed through my body causing my dick to harden. It wasn't really that much of a stretch either, I was so turned on during the movie Oliver could've just said my name, and I would've been hard.

OLIVER

God, he was so sexy. Every time a moan escaped from him it sent me closer to the edge. I trailed kisses down his stomach and came to the button of his jeans. I unbuttoned them quickly and started tugging at them. He lifted his hips slightly in assistance and I pulled them completely off. The only thing that remained on him was his boxer shorts. I snapped the elastic teasingly and then stripped them off of him.

Raven laid there on my couch completely naked, he blushed slightly as my eyes admired his body. I looked at his eyes, those eyes that captured my heart, they trailed down his lean chest and then rested on his already hard cock. I positioned myself in between his legs and spread them slightly. I ran my hands over his soft, white thighs and then softly ran my fingers from his balls to the tip of his cock. He moaned and shivered at my touch. Slowly I lowered my face and slipped his hardness into my mouth.

Raven tasted so good. I'd never thought about giving a guy head before, it had never entered my mind. I wasn't exactly gay, there was just something about him that made me want to do these things to him. I bobbed my head up and down, my hands spreading his legs from the back of his knees.

15

"Fuuuck that feels good." Raven moaned,

I continued sucking and bobbing on his dick and brought one of my hands to fondle his balls.

"If you do that then I don't think I'm going to last much longer."

I stopped sucking long enough to smile up at him and say, "Don't worry, you'll be cumming a lot more than just this time tonight."

Raven nodded his head and moaned again as I continued to suck on his cock. I could tell he wasn't going to last much longer, his hips were starting to buck up, almost as if he was trying to fuck my mouth.

"Oh no, Oliver, stop. I'm going to come!" He yelled trying to pull me away from his quivering member. But I wasn't having it. I was longing to know what it would taste like to have his juices dripping down my throat. I continued sucking until Raven tensed underneath me and released his load deep down my throat. I swallowed greedily lasting every drop he had to offer.

5

RAVEN

I watched as Oliver swallowed my load and licked his lips. I just couldn't get my fill of this guy bending over me. I started to sit up.

"Where do you think you're going?" Oliver asked, his tone was sarcastic but it had a sad undertone to it that almost broke my heart.

"It's my turn," I said, the lust evident in my voice. I leaned forward and pushed him back against the couch. I got up and he turned toward me. You wouldn't have noticed much wrong with him if it hadn't been for the dick now becoming obvious in his jeans. I leaned up to kiss his full lips and taste that sweet nectar that was Oliver Miller. Our tongues explored each other's mouths and he slightly sucked on my tongue sending waves of pleasure down my spine, making my cock twitch. I broke the kiss first, breathless, and began my inspection of his godlike body. I trailed my tongue down his body from his collarbone and stopped at his nipples. I captured one inside my mouth and the other with my fingers. Oliver caught his breath with a hiss. I swirled my tongue around his pearl-like nipples and slightly dug my teeth into them. My fingers worked their own magic. I rolled his nipple in between my thumb and index finger. I gave it a pinch and I felt Oliver's cock give a slight twinge. I switched, now giving his right nipple the undivided attention of my mouth. I applied suction to his nipple and flicked my tongue over the hard bud. He laced his fingers into my hair. My hands then began memorizing the rock hard crevices of his muscles. I brought myself down to my knees and kissed and licked down his abs. His breathing was becoming ragged. Oliver grabbed me by the shoulders and tossed me back onto the couch. He leaned me over the back of it and began massaging my ass. His thumb lightly brushed over my asshole and then a finger slowly pried its way inside. It didn't hurt - it caused a shock wave of pleasure that made my balls tense. Oliver lifted one of my legs up as he knelt down and licked the space beneath my hole.

"Mmmmmm" I moaned.

The pressure Oliver applied with his tongue made me shiver. I gripped the fabric of the couch underneath me. My cock pulsed with every lick. It seems like Oliver had found another one of my sweet spots that even I didn't know was that sensitive.

A second finger worked its way into my ass. Oliver's fingers and mouth hit my pleasure spot simultaneously from two angles. My cock strained and leaked pre-cum. My legs began to shake as Oliver's fingers began fucking my ass faster.

"Ahh! Oh, fuck! Fuck!"

It felt so good I was fighting back tears. My stomach muscles tensed and shuddered in tandem with the rhythmic massage. I started writhing against the couch. My toes began to curl, I arched my back and gave stilted gasps.

"Ah! I can't take it anymore!"

Just then a third finger spread my hole even wider. I could feel the penetration in excruciating detail: the pressure against my hole, the fold of my flesh separating, the fingers piercing my delicate insides. And yet it felt so good I couldn't even gather my thoughts enough to protest the intrusion, and honestly I really didn't want to.

"Ngh! Oliver, please!"

"Say, 'Fuck me, please.' Then you can come, baby. I wanna hear you say it."

"Ah, uhnnn!"

Oliver cupped my balls.

"Ahhhh!"

"Come on, baby. Say it."

Both of Oliver's hands tormented me with immense pleasure as his fingers fucked my ass and his tongue lapped upward into my asshole. He fucked my ass with unyielding fingers. My cock began to spasm as I came. My thighs trembled and goosebumps appeared all over my skin. I collapsed against the couch as my orgasm finished and tried to catch my breath. Then I said the words he wanted to hear most.

"Fuck me."

"What did you say?" Oliver asked, not attempting to hide the pleasure in his voice.

"Fuck me, please," I said as my cock began to harden again. I couldn't believe that I could say anything so shameless and eager. It was like someone else was causing the words to flow out of my mouth. But he wanted it. I heard Oliver remove his pants and underwear behind me. The sound of his belt loosening and the denim hitting the floor only caused me to become harder in anticipation.

Slowly at first but then more forcefully, Oliver's cock pushed into me. I winced slightly but then succumbed to the immense pleasure as he began fucking my tight hole. My hole stretched without pain, and the pleasurable feelings inside me became amplified as Oliver's cock pushed deeper and harder into me.

"Uhhh!"

I put my head down and arched my back displaying my ass for him as he fucked me. The deeper Oliver pressed into me the greater the ecstasy. My cock strained against the couch as the friction from being fucked hard brought me closer to the edge.

"Oliver! Ahh - yes!"

Oliver rammed into me now, and all I could do was squirm and beg for more. My cries seemed to add fuel to his lustful fire. Oliver stabbed into my ass with his huge cock as I writhed in pleasure with every thrust.

The pleasure reached a fast crescendo as my cock contracted with a powerful orgasm. I screamed as it caused me to shake violently. I breathed heavily and Oliver sat down next to me, his cock still hard.

OLIVER

I watched as Raven leaned back against the couch and tried to catch his breath. I watched him until he met my eyes and then looked down at my still hard cock. He licked his lips and then bit at his bottom lip. He slowly crawled towards me and slowly brought his lips to mine. Our kiss was electric. If I was tired before, I wasn't anymore. It was as if I had just been dead and the doctor applied the paddles to me, instant resuscitation. As we kissed I felt him shifting on the couch and slowly he straddled me. Without breaking our kiss, he eased my dick into his ass.

Raven was straddling my lap while facing me. I grabbed his ass and tightened my grip and pushed deeper into him.

"Ahh!" Raven moaned.

I watched him as his nipples hardened, he arched his back, and his dick hardened. His cock oozed a glistening droplet of pre-cum.

"Does it hurt?" I asked.

"Ah - no. It feels . . . feels so good. Ahh!"

"Raven. . . Ah!" I said barely able to get his name out through the onslaught of pleasure. I closed my eyes in an attempt to keep myself from coming before Raven had.

"Ahh! Uh! Yeah?" He said through gritted teeth as he rode me.

"I love you."

I opened my eyes when he didn't respond right away and he had stopped riding me. I could still feel the walls of his asshole clenching around me, but the missing friction caused me to be startled. When I opened my eyes I saw the look of complete shock on Raven's face as well as the cutest blush I had ever seen on a guy's face.

"I . . . I love you, too." He spoke each word as if one might break. I couldn't keep myself from smiling as I leaned in and kissed him.

I grabbed Raven's waist and held him in place as I thrust upwards into his soft, white ass cheeks. Our proclamation had sent a surge of energy into me.

"Ah! Wait!"

Raven's feet began to lose their grip on the sofa as I plowed into him, but I held him still. My hips slammed up against his ass. Each thrust felt like hot pleasure pouring over my cock. My cock pulsed on the edge of orgasm. Raven's face began to contort as his own orgasm approached. I reached down and began to stroke his cock in my hand as I fucked his ass.

"Ah! Stop!"

"Does it hurt?" I asked, concerned. Maybe I misread his signs of pain as pleasure.

"Don't . . . !" He yelled his breaths becoming ragged.

"What? You don't like it when I fondle you as I fuck the shit out of your ass, babe?" I asked.

"Just . . . ngh -"

I reached up and my thumb and index finger closed over a nipple and tugged. Raven angled his chest away.

"I . . . I can't take it. Fuck me harder! Make me come!"

"Sorry, Raven. I don't want you to come yet." I said seductively as I ran my hands down his chest and over his stomach.

My fingers coiled around his cock while my thumb caressed his slit.

Raven's stomach muscles jolted.

"Ahh!"

I mashed his tip with a circular thumb massage. Raven grabbed my wrist and tried to pull my hand away, but I held his cock tight and continued my torturous assault. He winced and jerked each time my thumb made a cycle. Every jerk he made allowed me to penetrate deeper into his ass.

"Ahh! Ah! Stop it!"

"Come on, babe. Watch yourself cum."

"Ngh!"

I focused my eyes on his cock and said, "Look."

Raven lowered his head with an agonizing face of pleasure. I squeezed my fist around his shaft. Raven tried to catch his breath, but I resumed thrusting up into him hard. I pumped his cock in tandem with my hips. All he could do was cling to me and cry out. A gush of white cum erupted from his cock.

"Ahhh!"

I massaged his balls as I continued to fuck him. I picked him up and laid him against the coach and with his leg over my shoulder, continuing to fuck him. I fucked him harder until our skin began to slap. I watched Raven as he grasped frantically to get a hold of something to brace himself against. His nails dug into the couch's cushion. I felt the tingling of pleasure spread from my balls to the tip of my dick as I slammed into Raven.

"Ah! Raven! I'm . . . I'm gonna cum." I said fighting to get the words out.

"Ahh! Uhhh! Me . . . me too! Come inside me, Oliver!" He said.

Those words sent me over the edge. Raven and I came simultaneously. Raven twitched as my load filled his insides. I collapsed on top of him and we both gradually faded off to sleep.

6

RAVEN

I woke up to the feeling of confusion. I didn't know where I was, but there was a certain amount of dread hidden in the back of my mind. Then the memories from last night flooded in. I face palmed. I can't believe I fucked him. I'm absolutely positive that I messed this entire thing up. I don't want a relationship. He isn't even gay. I really don't see this working out well for me. I tried to get off the couch, but there was something weighing down on my chest. I looked down to see the sleeping face of Oliver Miller. I slowly tried to dislodge myself from him but I was met with a sharp pain shooting through my backside. I might've gone a little overboard last night. I tried to move again, ignoring the pain, but was met with resistance. It was almost like I was anchored to the couch. God dammit, he fell asleep still inside of me. I moved myself upwards and off the couch slowly, careful not to wake him. I limped towards my clothes strewn on the floor. God, I was gross. There was sticky semen all over me, and I wasn't entirely sure if it was mine or his. I was tempted to use his shower, but I didn't want to run the risk of him waking up before I left. I pulled my shirt and jeans on, and called my sister Cassie.

I walked towards the front door while dialing, as soon as I closed the front door Cassie answered.

"Hello? Raven, is that you?" She said through the obvious grogginess of sleep. I looked at the time. It was five in the morning.

"Yeah, it's me. Do you think you can come get me? I fell asleep, and I need to get out of here fast."

Fifteen minutes later, Cassie's Altima pulled into Oliver's driveway, and then I was gone.

OLIVER

I woke to the sound of tires pulling out of the driveway. I sat up abruptly and looked around. I was completely naked and laying on the couch. My clothes were laying all over the floor and I had semen all over myself. I looked around, Raven's clothes weren't on the floor with mine anymore.

"Raven?" I yelled, my voice echoing slightly off the walls of my empty house. It was just me and the furniture. Now if only this was a scene from Beauty and the Beast, then I'd have someone here to share my misery with. Was I just a one night stand to him? The answer to that was as obvious as Raven's absence. I got up and walked to the shower, I had to get the shame of the experience off of me. I had told him I loved him. He said that he loved me, so why did he leave?

The hot water cascaded over my body and I began to scrub the cement-like semen off of my groin and chest. Memories from last night flood my mind. I thought of how good it felt to thrust my cock into his ass and the taste of him as I lapped at his hole. The sound of his cries of pleasure echoed inside my mind. He was gonna be a bitch to get over. I felt a tingling sensation in my pelvic area and looked down. God dammit, I was hard just thinking about him.

I reached down and stroked my now hard member. Thoughts of Raven as he rode me the night before flooded my mind and I jerked my dick faster. Each memory sent a wave of pleasure down my spine and through my cock. The feeling as he teased my nipples and licked my abs sent a shiver through me. The moment he said, "I love you, too." I shuddered and came hard at the thought of him sharing my feelings.

I finished washing my body and then went back out into the living room, the play screen from the movie we watched last night still playing on the TV. I plopped myself down onto the couch, closed my eyes, and tried to forget last night.

The more I tried to forget about Raven the more I got angry at my memories of last night. Why did he leave? Did he even mean it when he told me he loved me? Did I mean it when I said I loved him? Why did I even say that? I just got caught up in the moment but I don't feel like I lied either.

7

RAVEN

I've been on edge all morning. I look over my shoulder as I walk down the halls, I peek around corners, and I even changed lunch tables. So far I haven't run into him yet, but it's only the third period. I don't know how long I'm going to be able to keep this up, maybe I'll transfer colleges. I arrived at my classroom and eased myself into my usual seat in the back of the classroom. I put in my headphones and resumed my normal routine, almost as if last night never happened, and I had never gotten to know Oliver Miller. It wasn't until halfway through the class that shit started to go wrong.

I sat there, not really listening to the lecture that was being given when he walked in. I sensed him before I actually saw him. It was like a cold chill went down my spine, but it wasn't like, "Oh, that was scary," type of chill. Weirdly enough it was like the downhill fall of a roller coaster. My stomach flipped, goosebumps made their way up my arms, and I shivered at the feeling. I had to try my hardest to not get my hardest. When I felt the chill I turned towards the door and watched as Oliver started talking to my professor. I stared, not registering the conversation until he jerked his head in my direction. I unplugged my headphones in order to listen.

"I need Raven Weber. Coach Henderson needs us for a swim team meeting." Oliver said smoothly.

My professor mumbled something about how sports always get precedent over education and agreed to me leaving the class. Not bothering to fact check him or even notice that I was obviously not a swimmer or any type of athlete what-so-ever.

I slowly stood and walked out the door. I couldn't exactly rely on Mrs. Burns to understand how sports teams worked. Just last week she allowed this one guy named Tristan to leave when the women's bowling team was called to leave early. First of all, Tristan is a boy; second of all he plays no sports, absolutely none, and everyone knows this, and yet she still lets him leave without asking any questions.

As soon as the door closed, Oliver grabbed my arm and dragged me out of the school into the parking lot.

"Um, Oliver? What the hell's going on?" I asked in a shaky voice. He had been silent the entire walk and it was starting to scare me. But as the words escaped from my mouth I regretted them. Oliver stopped abruptly and turned toward me with so much fire in his eyes that I no longer wondered what hell looked like. I now knew what Oliver Miller looked like angry, and I didn't like it. But just as I thought that he might hit me, his lips crashed against mine. I felt like giving in and just melting into him, but then I remembered who I had been avoiding this entire morning. I spent so much time and effort trying to avoid him, and yet when he came and pulled me out of class I didn't even say a word of protest. I just let him drag me down the hallway. And he was kissing me in the middle of the college quad.

As these realizations ripped through me I pushed hard against Oliver's chest. Our lips separated and we glared angrily at each other.

OLIVER

"I knew it! You've been avoiding me!! What the fuck?!" I said as Raven and I glared at each other.

"'What the fuck?' You know we are at school right? This is not the place for this! And who said I was avoiding you!?"

"Don't give me that shit!! At first, I just thought, 'Well maybe he had to go get stuff from his house.' But then I saw you sit at another table when you saw me sitting at your usual table. I fucking saw you! You aren't exactly sneaky. Now you have to tell me; what is going on? What do you actually feel for me; because last night you told me you loved me, but then you weren't there this morning and you've been avoiding me all day? I think I deserve an answer seeing as how I was the one left in the dark." I breathed in for a moment seeing as how I said all this in one breath and waited for Raven's response in silence. Knowing him, as soon as he got the chance he would attack and make me think I was imagining it all. I stared at him with a fire burning in my eyes.

"Oh, you're done? It's finally my turn? Fantastic. Now first thing, I never said I wanted to go out with you. I was basically forced to come to your house, so I don't exactly count that as a date. Second of all, yes I've been avoiding you. Why? Because you were a one-night stand, plain and simple. Yes, I will admit that I was attracted to you, that's why I slept with you. That; however, does not mean that I'm in love with you. The fact that I said 'I love you' the other night has a simple explanation. If I had ignored you, or not said it back, you would've pulled out and that would've been awkward. In all honesty, this is your fault. Why the hell did you tell me you loved me when we had just met, we were on the first date. If you can even call it that. And in the middle of sex. That's fucking stupid! How did you expect me to react? You scared me away before we even started going out!! It would've been better for you if you had just left me alone. Since you didn't get it the first time, I'll tell you again. Leave me alone, Oliver. Go back to your popularity and friends, I'm no good for you."

"In what way are you not good for me, Raven? Is it the way just being next to each other makes me feel at home? Maybe it's the way, sexually, we fit together perfectly? Explain to me! I don't need you to be perfect, Raven. I don't need you to be anyone other than you!" I exclaim throwing my hands around excitedly.

"YOU KNOW NOTHING ABOUT ME! HOW WOULD YOU KNOW IF I'M PERFECT THE WAY I AM?" I scream. Why am I doing this? I don't want to hurt him.

8

Raven

"Leave me alone, Oliver. I'm no good for you." These words tasted like acid as I said to them. I didn't actually want to say them, but I knew it was true. Oliver and I are not the same no matter how much he thinks we are. It would be better if he just left me behind. That way it won't be as painful when he comes to the realization himself and leaves me when I let my guard down.

I waited until Oliver turned and left, his face turning red, before I started to cry.

I couldn't go back to class now, so I left. I walked home and collapsed as soon as the door to my room closed. As I cried the cruel words that I told him echoed in my mind, each one stabbing into my heart.

I don't know how long it was until I heard a knock at the door. I walked to the door and slowly opened it to see Oliver standing on the other side.

"What are you doing here?" I asked, thoroughly confused.

"You didn't go back to class after we talked, I got worried." He looked at me a little closer and said, "What's wrong? Why are your eyes all red?"

"That doesn't matter. Are you gonna come in or not?" I said while wiping my face.

Oliver walked through the door and stood there awkwardly. I observed his face and noticed a red tinge around his blue eyes. Had he been crying? He looked older now almost as if within the last few hours he had aged twenty years. His jet black hair now seemed to have lost its sheen and was looking like a black t-shirt that had been washed too many times.

"What did you want to say?" I asked. I already knew the answer, but I asked anyway. He wanted to talk to me, possibly even yell, about what I said to him earlier today. But then he surprised me by saying something completely unexpected.

"I'm sorry. I didn't know that I forced you to come to my house, actually now that you mention it, I did know. I didn't want you to turn me down, so I just didn't give you a choice. Then I couldn't hold myself back after we watched the movie. To tell you the truth, I've wanted you since the day I first saw you. I didn't know it at the time but I've been thinking a lot about what you said earlier. I'm pretty sure I'm bisexual, and I don't really know what to do with this information. All I do know is that I want you. All of you, but right now I'm willing to take what you'll give me. Even if it's just a friendship" he winces at the taste of those words coming out of his mouth. He obviously did NOT want to be my friend. "You would always sit away from everyone, and it made me want to get closer to you."

He stood there for a moment more and then said, "Well that's all I had to say. So if you never want to see me again, I'll leave." He turned towards the door and I stepped in front of him involuntarily. It didn't matter how much my head said that I didn't love him, my heart and body were adamant that I did.

"Wait ... Stay."

OLIVER

The moment he said those words I couldn't control myself, I leaned forward to kiss him. But I stopped as soon as I saw the look in his eyes.

"I'm sorry, I'm doing it again, aren't I? But it's hard for me to hold back when you're just so cute." I said as I realized my mistake. The whole reason I was here was to apologize for forcing myself on him the first time, and now I'm doing it all over again.

At the sound of my apology, his face began to soften. He turned to walk toward the kitchen and asked me if I liked Italian food.

"Yeah, I do. You mean like pizza and spaghetti, right?

He smiled at me. "Yeah, stuff like that." Then he said. "Oliver?"

"Yes?"

"You're pretty fucking cute yourself." He smiled.

I knew that I was blushing and I felt like a total idiot. I stared at my shoes. I mean I knew that I wasn't like the Hunchback of Notre Dame or anything but that complement just kinda threw me. Finally, I glanced over at Raven, he hadn't taken his eyes off me. He reached over, grabbed my hand, and brought me into the kitchen.

Raven's house was a large three bedroom with a living room, dining area, laundry, kitchen, and some sort of den area. The decorating was a kind of a pleasing blend of modern and Gothic, it had a very weird comfortable feeling, almost as if it was perfect for him.

I asked him where his bathroom was, he directed me to it, and I went inside. I was a little nervous, I'd never been inside Raven's house before. After I had composed myself I walked back out of the bathroom.

I walked into the kitchen where Raven was fixing spaghetti. As soon as I saw him in an apron I got a hard-on. I tried desperately to hide it, I didn't want him to think I was gonna force myself on him again.

Raven saw me walk in and said, "Come here. Just keep stirring this sauce, he put a long wooden spoon in my hand. I'm gonna take a quick shower, but I'll be right back." He looked down at where my dick was tensing against my jeans and smiled. He kissed me quickly on the mouth. His kiss sent a jolt through my body setting every cell on fire. Raven's voice was kind of sexy now that I thought about it. It was a voice that could threaten, cajole, seduce, and every time I heard it knocked me off my feet. There was something about this kid that made me want to drop to my knees. Raven was dangerous.

Raven came out of the bathroom wearing a pair of pale gray sweatpants and a black t-shirt. He was an unbelievable sight and I'm sure that I was just starring the entire time. I couldn't think of anything I wanted more in a boyfriend than what I was seeing.

"Are you ready to eat?

"Huh?" I said snapping out of my daydreams.

"You're drooling," Raven stated.

I swore internally as I wiped away my drool. I coughed nonchalantly and said, "Um so where did you learn to cook this?"

"I started making this when I lived in Italy when I was younger. My mom kinda gave me the recipe and I've eaten like a zillion pounds of it over the years." He smiled that kind of half-smile that said there was a lot more to come under the right circumstances.

He had started serving the dinner, setting out salads, and bread but he stopped and looked at me nervously. I stood, looked into his eyes, and said, "Nothing, and I mean absolutely nothing is going to happen unless you want it to."

I looked down for a minute, then looked into his eyes again. "I wouldn't ever do anything to hurt you." Then I gave an embarrassed little laugh and then more loudly. "As I've said before, I'm a good guy."

He leaned over, steadying himself with a hand on my shoulder, and kissed me. "I believe you....about everything but especially about you being a good guy."

I pulled away.

"I think we better eat before things get outta hand....like I hope they will later."

Then. "Just kidding....no pressure." God, Raven has the most beautiful mouth. Goddamn these perverted thoughts!

RAVEN

Finally, dinner was done. I poured us a couple of cups of coffee and suggested we take them into the living room where I set them on the coffee table. I looked back at Oliver.

"Still got your hard-on?"

"It comes and goes. No pun intended." He teased.

Oliver sat on the sofa kind of slouched down, his legs spread a bit and asked, "Why don't you come here?"

He held out his hand. I took it and he pulled me slowly to his lap. It was awkward for a moment but I finally decided it would be easiest to straddle his lap facing him. My knees were against his hips and my butt was basically over his cock. This felt natural. Like we fit perfectly together.

Oliver ran his hands up my thighs and then let them rest on my butt. Then he looked at me and said, "You know you're amazing, right?"

"Ha Ha. Yeah right." I said my voice was full of sarcasm.

"You are! How don't you see that?" He ran his hands up my back and touched his forehead to my chest. He breathed in my scent and then nuzzled against my chest. "I could stay like this forever."

"I know right? It's kind of comfortable." I said smiling as I looked down at him.

He sighs and then says, "I should probably go home."

I frown. "Why?" Weren't we having a good time? Was he bored already?

"Well, I want to go slower. I've been at a sprint this entire time and I need to slow down. I don't have to go fast with you and I want you to know you can be comfortable with me. So I'm gonna head home before I jump your bones and then I will see you tomorrow. Maybe give it a day or two and then we can go out again."

I pout. I don't want to take it that slow though. "Do we have to take it slow?"

"I think that'd be a good idea. Trust me, I don't want to take it slow either. Honestly, you just sitting here is doing dangerous things to my body. So I'm gonna get up," he says as he moves me off his lap, "and head to my Mom's house."

He leans closer to me and whispers in my ear, "That way I'm not tempted to just come right back."

I wrap my arms around his neck and give him a quick kiss. "Drive safe."

He heads to the door and waves before it closes behind him. The sound of his car pulling out of the driveway just makes my heartache for him to run back into my arms.

9

RAVEN

I haven't seen Oliver at all today. None of his usual staring at me while in my classes, no passing glances while in the halls, no tell-tale goosebumps of his stalking. Nothing. I don't think he's avoiding me because he said we would see each other today after he left last night. For all, I know he didn't even go to his classes today. Which is why I am where I am now. Stalking him outside his Environmental Biology course during my free period.

There he was, sitting in his usual spot right in front of the door, his head nodded to the music he was listening to. I felt as if my feet were glued to the floor, no matter how much I willed them to move they stayed still. His head stopped nodding and he slowly turned his head to meet my gaze. Then I saw his face as he noticed me standing there. He gave me a cocky smile as if he knew I'd show up eventually and gave me an air kiss from his seat. My face deadpans as he winks at me and turns his attention back to his textbook in front of him, bobbing his head to his music once again. Cocky bastard.

OLIVER

Throughout the whole class, I could feel a piercing gaze on me. Trailing all over me. I didn't mind it because I knew it was Raven being an adorable stalker from the hallway.

The bell sounds and I can't remember what the class was even about. That happened a lot. All I could do was think of Raven, his eyes, the way he spaces out, the way he hides behind his black bangs. I love how he walked confidently but still managed to keep his head low, almost as if he was trying to distance himself from everyone. His gaze didn't help either. My mind just kept telling me he was there, just out of reach.

I pulled my lunch out of my locker and then it slammed shut. To my displeasure, it was Alyssa Davis. She never gives up, does she? Alyssa has been following me around, begging me for a date, since I was a freshman. I get it. She thinks I'm 'special'. But she doesn't understand that I'm not interested. I guess she just can't take a hint.

"Alyssa. Hello. What do I owe this displeasure?" I ask disdainfully.

"Well I have some time in my schedule today after school and I've decided you're the lucky guy I want to spend it with." I sigh, here we go again.

"Enlighten me. Why is it that you just can't seem to take no for an answer? I have been very clear to every person to ever ask me out that I am not interested. I'm not playing hard to get. I'm. Just. Not. Interested."

"Well my little riptide," she says as she reaches up and runs her fingers through my hair causing my skin to crawl, "If anyone could have you . . . . then I wouldn't want you. The fun is all in the chase as they say."

"Well," I say shaking her hand off me, "I'm not interested. I'm actually in a relationship now."

She scoffs indignantly, "What the hell, Oliver? You literally say every day how you don't want to be in a relationship and then turn around and get in a relationship. That makes no sense! What makes this new girl better than me? I'm totally hotter than her!"

"You realize you aren't the pinnacle of beauty right? I don't base all of my relationships on whether or not they are hotter than you."

"So she ISN'T hotter than me!"

I facepalm, "You're missing the point. That isn't what makes me pick someone. And for the record," I say as I lean in close, "They get me harder than you ever could."

Her face turns red as she processes my words. I couldn't tell if it was from embarrassment from my choice of words or if it was from anger. I didn't really care though. I continued walking to the cafeteria thinking that had solved all my problems.

I enter the cafeteria but before I can locate Raven, Alyssa rushes into the middle of the cafeteria in front of me yelling, "So you're gonna choose this WHORE who was willing to sleep with you, probably on the first date, over ME!?"

I look down and then back up fire burning in my eyes. I feel my anger build up against my dam of patience and it cracks, leaving the tsunami of rage to break free.

"The only WHORE I see here is you! You've been chasing me for almost three years, throwing yourself at my feet! It didn't matter WHO I was already dating, you'd be there to throw yourself at me once again! Why is it that when a female says no all guys are supposed to bow down and back off, but the same courtesy isn't given to men? I have NEVER expressed ANY interest in you. But obviously my nice way of turning you down just saying 'No thanks, I'm good.' Wasn't fucking good enough! I told you I'm in a relationship. I don't want to date, hang out, talk to, have sex with, or have any general type of association with you. Now I didn't want to turn you down like this but it seems like the only way you are going to get it through that thick skull of yours. I have not been nor will I ever be attracted enough in order to want to do anything with you."

"Who even is this bitch? Tell me! Or does she not even exist? What's this so-called goddess who's so much more attractive than me?"

Waves of anger roared in my ears. "Alright. We're still doing this? Okay, fine. They are sexy first thing in the morning, tired as hell. I've watched them down three cups of coffee before their first class while yawning beautifully. Their black hair is always a mess, never combed, and god does it look sexy as hell. Brown eyes that I could get lost in all day, and a body that gets me harder than a rock. And they are far from a whore," I emphasized that word as I stared piercingly at her. "Honestly, all of the advances have been from me. They aren't concerned with popularity, theirs or mine, and I'd do anything to be in their arms right now. Real enough for you?" I didn't wait for her answer as I went to head towards my seat.

As I faced the other way I felt a gaze again. Despite my better judgment I looked in the direction of the gaze. To my surprise those brown eyes I love so much were watching me intently from the other side of the cafeteria. How long had he been watching? His face was slowly turning red and he got up and ran out.

10

RAVEN

I stopped to catch my breath when I could no longer hear the plodding of Oliver's feet chasing after me. 'God, I'm out of shape.' I gasp as I struggle to take in the much-needed air. I don't know why I ran. It isn't like they would know that it was me he was talking about per se but more so that when we became public then it would be obvious that I was the one he had been talking about.

My embarrassment at his words bubbled up to the surface again, but that wasn't all I was feeling. There was a foreign feeling of jealousy and rage when I saw her throwing herself at him. 'He's mine!' Raged the beast within me. She had touched him, I could tell. She made him uncomfortable. I didn't like what this feeling was doing to me. I felt like a completely different person.

"Don't worry. I'm sure he'll come to his senses eventually." I heard a female voice say from the hallway around the corner.

"It doesn't fucking matter, Tammy! He said that shit in front of the whole fucking campus!" Alyssa hisses towards the other girl who apparently was named Tammy.

"So, then what are you gonna do? It's obvious he's more serious about this new girl than he was when he was dating Anna. I don't think you'll be able to get between them. You don't even know who this girl is, so it's not like you can blackmail her into dumping him." Alyssa turned her fiery glare on the other girl who I had never seen before. But then again I didn't really try to learn people's names.

"That's where you guys come in. Find her. I don't care how you do it but find out everything about who he's been spending time with. Once you do that, I'll take care of it from there. He will be mine." Alyssa growls as she slams her locker shut and flounces off down the hallway towards me. I scurry to hide just in time as she passes me, breathing a sigh of relief.

"Who are you hiding from?" I practically jump out of my skin at the sound of Oliver's voice.

"Jesus fuck!" I scream out and I fall against the lockers next to me.

"You wouldn't have been trying to hide from me, were you?" He asks skeptically.

"No, fuck. You scared the shit out of me. I was eavesdropping." I explain.

"Oh really? Spill. What'd you hear?" Oliver asks excitedly.

"Alyssa is basically putting a bounty on my head. Or rather my assumed head since she doesn't know who I actually am." I say with a shrug.

Oliver sighs, "You mean she STILL isn't getting the hint to just leave me the fuck alone?"

"Nope and now my ass is on the line." I look at Oliver for a second and feel my possessiveness rise to the surface again. "Did she touch you?"

"What? I haven't been involved with her at all, Raven."

"No, I mean did she touch you at all. Anything."

"She touched my hair. And honestly, it made my skin crawl." I reach up and run my fingers through his sleek hair, my hand lingering at his cheek. Oliver leans into my hand with a slight smile on his lips. I caress his cheek with the pad of my thumb and he moves his lips to kiss the palm of my hand. I smile lovingly. Oliver looks from left to right and then leans into me against the wall and gives me a lingering kiss that I don't have the strength to pull away from. His lips were so soft against mine and they moved with such expert ability. Oliver ended the kiss with a peck and then another on my forehead lingering for just a moment.

"I'm sorry I embarrassed you." He apologized, pulling me into a hug.

"I'm not upset about it. Only embarrassed in the aspect of 'a body that gets me harder than a rock' because if we ever become public at school that'll be awkward for everyone to know that A. I slept with you on the first date. And B. That not only did I fuck you but apparently it was so good that you switched teams." I say as I pull away from the hug. As I do I notice a glimpse of brunette hair as a girl I recognize as the one Alyssa was talking to that I didn't know. Fuck. Well, my anonymity didn't last long.

"So am I allowed to take you out this weekend?" Oliver whispers in my ear. The sensation sent a chill down my spine as his warm breath brushed over my ear.

"Only if you stay the night afterward," I say with my brown eyes darkening to almost black with lust. Oliver's blue eyes darken turning almost slate in color.

"I don't know. Are you ready for what that'll entail?" He asks with a cocky grin on his lips.

"Definitely."

"Well, we know one thing for sure now. I wasn't lying with what I said earlier."

I look at him questioningly, "What do you mean?"

"Everything about you gets me rock hard." He says almost with a growl as he leans his erection into me.

I blush crimson red, which stands out even worse on my pale skin.

11

RAVEN

'I have a lot of work to do'. I thought to myself as I looked around at my house. The winter solstice was in two days, the darkest day of the year, and I hope you know what that means. My dad was coming home. I had a total of thirty hours to clean the house and figure out a way of telling my dad about Oliver.

To be honest, it probably wouldn't come as much of a surprise to him. I mean, I was raised mostly by my mom and sister, no father figure around to make sure I came to that heterosexual conclusion. But I don't blame my family, I was born like this. My small frame basically made it to where the only type of girl who would look good with me was a 4 foot 8 inches tall, dark-haired, brown-eyed, goth girl with a small build. That is extremely specific and I am sure there aren't many of them. My appearance basically made it obvious that I was going to end up as a lean hot guy's bottom lover. And look at what happened.

But I'm okay with the outcome, Oliver is perfect. I mean, he could have a little more in the intelligence department, but he isn't stupid. Just a little slow. Kind of like he just had a little too much water in his head. I loved him anyways though.

I walked around the house and picked up clothes and threw away the trash. I looked around the house. I had a lot of work to do. I hadn't done any dishes, laundry, or cleaning of any kind this last week.

I've been a little preoccupied with a certain sexy swimmer.

Down the hall, I heard the sound of the front door opening and closing. Then the sound of footsteps.

"Raven? Are you home?" It was Cassie.

"In the kitchen!" I yelled back.

Cassie walked around the corner into the kitchen and stopped abruptly, her eyes wide.

"Holy shit, Raven! I was gone for two days and look what you did to the house!"

"I know, I know. I'm working on it! Are you going to help me, or just stand there and stare at it like it's a crime scene?" I asked, gesturing to the mess as I took out the trash and replaced it with a fresh bag.

Cassie, how do I describe Cassie? My dad met her mom when she was on Rumspringa, the Amish holiday where they go out into modern society to see if they want to return. She met my dad, they discovered more than just technology together and ended up getting pregnant with Cassie. Cassie was born back inside the Amish community. Once it came time for her holiday - she showed up at our door, went to her own college, met Frank, they started dating, and one thing led to another - Cassie never returned to the Amish community. It was funny though, watching her stare into store windows at TVs and anything else modern. She still asks questions about modern society.

My dad owns several mining corporations, as well as several mausoleums and morgues. The mausoleums are under the name Hades Afterlife Incorporated, and the mining corporations are under the name Pluto's Sphere, Dad's will says that once Cassie graduates from college she will inherit Pluto's Sphere, and once I graduate from college I get Hades Afterlife Incorporated. Cassie always jokes that she and I make up the two hemispheres of "Pluto's Sphere," you know from Greek and Roman mythology? I get death and she gets the riches.

My dad is half Greek and half Italian. He was born in Greece and then later his family moved to Rome. So he felt like paying homage to their gods. Italy was actually where he met my mom, she was the daughter of an Italian dignitary.

Cassie bent down and started picking up trash. She threw away paper plates, empty bottles, and several other things.

I was about to bring out the trash when Cassie said, "Raven, what the fuck is this?"

I turned around, not expecting what she was holding.

It was a used condom.

"Ummmm, that's not mine," I said defensively as both our faces turned scarlet.

"I didn't even know you had a girlfriend!"

"I don't," I said bluntly.

"Don't tell me you've been fucking randoms!"

Shit.

"You better hope Dad doesn't find out."

"Find out about what?" asked a voice from behind us.

Double shit.

We both froze and Cassie dropped the condom. I stepped on it and moved it closer to me, very subtly. Smooth.

45

No one said anything. We all just stared at each other, then Dad started looking around the kitchen. First, he noticed the trash bag at my feet. Then, he noticed the unwashed dishes in the sink.

He looked back at me and Cassie and asked once more, "Find out about what?"

"Ummmm," I said smartly.

Then Cassie came to my rescue and answered, "About Raven's new girlfriend!"

Yes, Cassie saved me. She saved me from the boiling water and then threw me into the fire.

"Raven . . . has a girlfriend?" Dad asked with as much surprise as I had imagined. I didn't take offense to his tone. I just didn't look like the kind of guy who "had a girlfriend." And guess what . . . . I didn't. But that doesn't mean I told my dad that. I wasn't ready for the whole "I'm gay" conversation. I thought I still had 24 hours to get myself ready for that.

"Sure," I answered vaguely," I'm seeing someone."

Yes, the condom is forgotten.

Just don't use any specific pronouns and everything will be just fine.

"I'm going to need to meet her, of course. This girl might be a future owner of Hades Afterlife Incorporated after all. You should invite her over for dinner tomorrow."

"Can't they've got dinner with their family."

"Then on the solstice. It'd be nice to share one of our holidays with someone you love."

Damn.

"Alright. I'll talk to them after dinner."

"Good. Now, clean up this shit hole, it's disgraceful." He turned to leave the kitchen but then looked over his shoulder and said, "Oh, and Raven?"

"Yes, Dad?"

"Get your foot off that condom and throw it away, it's disgusting to have it in the kitchen."

Double Damn. I swear to God, he knows everything.

I pulled out my phone and found Oliver's phone in my contacts list. I was about to call him when my phone rang.

It was from Oliver. He's weird like that, he must know everything too.

"Hey, Babe. I was just about to call you. We gotta talk about something . . . " I left the kitchen and walked towards my bedroom.

12

OLIVER

"Dinner? That's funny, I was just about to ask you the same thing about tomorrow."

"But aren't you having dinner with your family at Jaxon's house tomorrow?" Raven asked through the phone.

"Yeah, I just figured that having you there would make it easier for me, and easier for them to accept. I mean, my mom and Paul will more than likely be chill with it, it's just my dad I'm worried about."

"Speaking of which. My dad wants to meet you."

"You told him already?" I asked, surprised.

"No, he thinks I'll be introducing him to my girlfriend. Ironically, I think I'm closer to being the girlfriend than you are."

I smiled at that, "No, Babe. You and I are all man. But that's how you like it, right?"

"Haha, you know it, Baby." His tone was off. I felt like I had flipped a switch inside Raven. His voice came out raspy, and it was almost as if I could hear his lust.

"Raven, what are you doing right now?"

"Cleaning the house. I was supposed to have it done before Dad got home and before we went out tonight."

"I suppose that's my fault somehow. I mean I have been occupying most of your time lately."

"Hmm, well. I'm almost done, so, why don't you come pick me up in fifteen minutes and we can get preoccupied together." He whispered seductively.

"Sounds like a plan to me. Are we gonna go out in public tonight or is this a private party?"

"Why do we have to choose? I'm game for all of the above."

"Okay, well let me just hop in the shower real fast. I just got back from the gym. I'll be there in fifteen minutes."

"Let's make it ten minutes. I need my daily dose of sexy."

Hmm, Raven sounded horny.

"I'll be right there." I hung up the phone and grabbed my keys, the shower forgotten.

RAVEN

Yes, I was horny. But it isn't my fault. Oliver spoiled me too much, and when we were apart I couldn't stand it. It was like he was cocaine and I was addicted. Boy was I addicted.

But who wouldn't be? He had everything that I could ever want in a boyfriend. He had the looks of limited - but still evident - intelligence, he had a kind heart, but best of all he had the stamina to keep up with my ever-hungry libido.

A libido that I was struggling to keep under control as we bought our tickets to see a movie about how a mother is murdered trying to protect her children. Later once the only surviving child grew up he was abducted, and the father goes on a quest to save his son. He also gets help from a mentally disabled female along the way.

Sounds great, right? That's what I said. It's fucking 'Finding Nemo in 3D'. But who was I to argue; it's Oliver's favorite movie, and I couldn't find anything better.

The only problem with going to see someone's favorite movie is: even though you might not be that interested, they are. And as the movie went on, and my boredom became more obvious, my libido began to get the best of me. The shitty part of that is: Oliver doesn't tolerate SHIT when 'Finding Nemo' is playing.

I tried to hold his hand: Shook it off.

I tried to lay my head on his shoulder: he shrugged me off.

I placed my hand on his knee: he picked it up and put it back by me.

Finally, I tried to kiss him: he said, "Seriously, Raven? During 'Finding Nemo'?"

Guess who isn't getting laid tonight . . . This guy.

It was when Dori and Marlin were inside the whale, that was when I got out of my seat, and onto my knees in front of him.

"Raven? What are you doing?"

"Don't worry about it," I said as I undid his zipper and pulled out his cock. He started to get a chub as I wrapped my hand around him.

"Raven, there are people here." He said looking around frantically.

"It's okay. It's dark, and there are only like ten people here. Just don't be too loud."

I gripped his shaft tighter, started to lick his balls, trying to moisten my mouth.

There was a salty taste that only turned me on more. His balls are pretty big. One after the other, I put them in my mouth, and enjoyed them there, giving each a gentle suck.

Despite what I was doing, Oliver's eyes never left the screen.

His cock was heavy in my hand. I licked and kissed my way down his length.

Realizing his dick was hardening slowly, I ran my tongue back over his balls and then up. When I reached the head, I opened wide and put the whole thing inside.

I felt so good in my mouth. At this semi stage, it fit just perfectly, but I knew that wouldn't last long. I decided to speed up the inevitable. I moved my head back and forth, slowly at first, and brought saliva to my mouth. With my wet lips, I applied a circle of pressure, enjoying the way a half-erect dick could be squeezed to shift its fullness around.

I glanced up quickly. Oliver's head was tilted back, his eyes shut. He breathed steadily, controlled. For now.

I went a little faster and slid my tongue over his head. His erection practically snuck up on me, hitting my gag reflex. Now that he was hard, I wanted to see his full glory. I came away to admire his throbbing Oliver's cock looked like it could take whatever it wanted by force. It was approximately seven inches, possibly eight depending on where you measured it from, and thick with a subtle curve to it. Perfect for reaching some great spots; which I had experience with first hand. My asshole turned sensitive. I wanted him inside.

I put my hand back around his shaft. It couldn't be squeezed now, it was too hard. With it in my mouth again, I moved up and down in sync with my hand. Oliver's breathing became louder. I kept going, steadily, and he pressed his back against the chair like the pleasure was too much to handle. I wanted to see how much he enjoyed it. I peered up his body. He was looking down at me now, watching intently.

"Damn, Raven. You look good on my dick."

My cock was becoming extremely uncomfortable, cramped in my jeans.

I gave a little laugh to his comment, but then I was back down on him.

I put only the head in my mouth as I began jerking him off fast. It was as if my mouth was his to use for shooting his load.

"Uhhhh, stop, I'm close." He moaned. I pulled away.

After he cooled down, I went back to sucking him. Glancing up, I saw him reclining his head as he had before. I sucked rhythmically, loving the warmth of his dick in my mouth, feeling a vein pulse against my upper lip.

Oliver opened his legs wider. I went faster. Up, down, up, down.

Close, he made me stop again, but I continued as soon as possible. My dick was so stiff it hurt.

I heard long and deep moans from Oliver and his legs spasmed a little. With the hand that wasn't around the base of his dick, I reached up and touched Oliver's abs. The muscles tensed.

Again, he got close. Then I was back at it. Now I sucked him hard and fast. Out of the corner of my eye, I saw him grip the armrests. Then he grabbed my head with one hand and did most of the work himself. I took back my hand from his abs and cupped his balls, massaging. He let loose a short gasp. Now with both hands, he gripped my hair and gave lusty, forceful thrusts into my mouth.

I felt completely like his toy. He used me so roughly I had no choice but to breathe through my nose. He just went at it as if he'd forgotten the movie, as well as the other people in the room. Then he moaned, "Fuck," quite loudly I might add. And his cum began to flood my mouth. I swallowed, looked up at him, and then licked my lips.

That's when I noticed all the people staring at Oliver. Thankfully, they hadn't noticed me.

"What? Didn't you people see them all just get stuck in the net?! I mean holy shit, this is intense! Swim down! Everybody, swim down! Come on, Dori! Just keep swimmin'. Just keep swimmin'." Oliver yelled realistically.

People gave him one more perplexed look and then returned to watching the movie.

"Wow, that was close," I whispered.

I guess we were still too attracted to each other to go out in public. But I'm okay with that.

13

OLIVER

Once we got back to my place Raven started stripping. I won't say that I didn't expect it, but it was a little fast even for us.

I walked up behind him, wrapped my arms around his waist, and asked, "Would you like to take a shower first?"

He nodded and I pulled him by the hand toward my bathroom.

In the shower, I turned him around towards the wall and began to soap him down. The suds trickled between his shoulder blades and down the small of his back to between his ass cheeks. My fingers followed the trail left behind, massaging, stroking, cleansing. He turned and I repeated my movements. But, on the way down, I paid special attention to his balls, gently squeezing and kneading them. My cock was standing up rigid but, with all the soap that was covering us, I couldn't tell what was pre-cum and what was soap.

Then, we swapped places. His hands did the same routine that I had just performed for him. But once he got to my cock, he knelt on the shower floor and brought his lips to my head. He gently sucked, his tongue just brushing my erection.

As soon as I could no longer stand it, we left the shower and didn't bother to dry much; we were both too aroused. Just wrapped in bath towels, we stumbled to my bed, fell on it and as he sucked me I sucked him, it was the classic "sixty-nine" that I had read so much about but had never tried, not even with a girl.

I pulled Raven off of me before I could cum and positioned him in doggy-style.

I began to stroke one of his cheeks with my cock.

I gripped his hips and ground my dick between his legs.

I spread his cheeks, placed my dick between then, squeezed them together, and thrust. I thrust into him five times before I pulled out. Earning a whimper from Raven.

I pulled his cheeks apart, licked two of my fingers, and then pressed them into Raven's hole. Using my spit for lube, I gently fingered him.

I pulled my fingers out gently and Raven reached back to try and direct them back inside, but I swatted his hand aside and inserted my hard cock.

It wasn't long before Raven began moving back and forth, sliding me further in and out of him. I let him take the lead for a while, but before long my urges got the better of me. And I began slamming into him.

Outside in the living room, I heard the door open and close. Then the TV turns on.

Dad was home. Hopefully, he wouldn't hear me and Raven's groans and sighs.

I pushed Raven's ass lower and flattened him to the bed. I climbed up behind him. I spread him wide open and fucked him deeper than before.

I pushed Raven's head down and dominated him, then I bit his lower back.

Shivers ran up and down Raven's body.

I bit his neck, stroked his thighs, and squeezed his ass. Then I thrust faster, building a rhythm. It felt so good I was afraid I'd accidentally spill my load.

The pleasure took control of me and I didn't care if my dad heard us anymore. I started doing him hard, propelling the bed into the wall with a bang, bang, bang.

"Ungh . . ." I whispered in Raven's ear. "It feels fucking amazing."

Then he whispered, "I'm gonna fucking cum."

Then I pressed him down and went for it. I could feel Raven's ass tensing around me. Again, and again, I filled him up. The sensations pushed Raven overboard and he came, a warm sticky mess spreading out between him and the bed. I came and moaned louder than I ever thought I had in my life.

"That was good." Raven expressed.

And of course, that was when the knock came at my door.

Shit.

RAVEN

I never knew how fast I could get dressed until I heard the knock on Oliver's bedroom door. I'm no expert, but I am pretty positive that I broke a fucking record.

It was his father.

"Yes?" Oliver yelled as he pulled on his clothes.

"Did I wake you up?" Asked his dad through the door.

"Naw, I've got a friend over so we were just playing video games."

"Oh, ok. Well, I just thought you had something to talk to me about. Your text from before seemed a little tense. So I figured I should come home and talk to you." That was when Oliver opened the door.

Now we just sat across from each other and waited for someone to start the conversation.

"I'm sorry. I don't believe I've met you before. My name is Fisher Seafarer, I'm Oliver's father." He held out his hand and I grasped it tentatively. Oliver's father looked nothing like what I thought he would, but that makes sense because I am often wrong. And, to be honest, his dad reminded me a lot of Oliver. Oliver had his dad's sea-green eyes and his same black hair. His dad was wearing Bermuda shorts in December, a short sleeve Hawaiian shirt, and brown sandals. He had laugh lines that told me that he laughed a lot and he smelt like salt water. The ocean wasn't exactly my favorite place but the way Oliver's dad smelt made me want to go there right now. Actually, now that I think about it, Oliver smelled like the ocean too. With a touch of chlorine from his swimming practices. But he smelt like a nice comforting sea breeze on a beautiful summer day.

"My name is Raven Weber."

Oliver decided that, instead of tomorrow, we would tell his dad that we were gay (and dating) today. That's my boyfriend. The man with the not-so-well-thought-out plans and the fly-by-the-seat-of-my-pants attitude.

"Umm, Dad? We have something to tell you."

"I'm all ears, Son."

"We, Raven and I, are gay. Together. As in seeing each other. As in dating. As in we love each other. As in I will literally die without him. As in - "

"Oliver, I think he gets it."

"Oh, sorry. I just didn't want you to misunderstand."

Mr. Seafarer nodded and said, "Well you made it very clear."

"Sooooo . . . . ?" We both waited in painful suspense for him to answer.

"Oh, it's fine. Greeks don't actually care about gender. It makes sense that you would at least end up bisexual. I mean just look at your cousin Solaris, you probably don't remember but there was this whole thing with this one guy that both he and his friend Coup liked. I don't quite remember what happened to them. But our family has never had issues with homosexuality in the past, I don't see why we would start now."

"Well, that was anticlimactic," I said letting the breath I had been holding escape.

Now we just had my dad to worry about. But he probably would say the same thing. He was half Greek, and even his Italian side - I mean Italians were known for being kinda loose. I don't think I have much to worry about. If anything it was Cassie. She was raised in an Amish society, they were literally old-fashioned. My only hope was that in the limited amount of time that she had been in modern society she had picked up a modern view on gay marriage.

14

OLIVER

Fucking fantastic. And that is with absolutely no sarcasm whatsoever. I couldn't have wished for our conversation to go any better than it had. But now I feel a little stupid about worrying too much. I mean, I wasn't there with the whole Solaris-is-bisexual thing but it had been a HUGE topic way back when. Not because of him being bi but because the guy he fell in love with ended up dying. Solaris was great at many things, he holds three championship titles in archery, but discus was never his sport and he refused to acknowledge that. The stray discus ended up bashing in the guy's head. It's a hell of a way to get dumped though.

Then again Solaris had a bad habit of falling in love with a lot of people. He even stole his half-sister Aphie's boyfriend, Adam. I don't think he's dating anyone now, let's just hope Raven isn't his type.

"Oliver! What should I wear?!" cried Raven from the other room.

"It's just dinner, Raven! You don't have to wear anything fancy! Just dress nice."

Then Raven walked out of the bedroom with a pair of black denim skinny jeans on, a v-neck shirt, covered by a black coat with the sleeves rolled up, completed by a chain necklace with a skull at the end of it. All of the breath was knocked out of me.

"Damn, babe. You look hot. We might not make it to dinner."

Raven blushed slightly and said, "I just got dressed, you can unwrap me later. . . . . Is that seriously what you're wearing?"

I looked down at my outfit. I had on black slacks, a black vest over a white button-down shirt, and just for a little color, I added a sea-green tie that matched my eyes. I thought I looked fucking awesome.

"What's wrong with what I'm wearing?" I asked, confused.

"You look too good, I'm not going to be able to focus. And you make me look like shit." I laughed at his response.

"Impossible. You're too sexy to ever look like shit. Not to mention that I already told you that you looked hot as hell."

He sighed and nodded slowly. "You're right. I look great, you look great. Everything is going to be fine. I'm just nervous for no reason. You're Greek, no one cares about genders there. Everything is going to be fine. They are going to like me, right? What's not to like - "

"Raven, you're hyperventilating. Calm down. You'll be fine." I reached over and hugged him close to me. He still had that same cinnamon smell that I remembered from the first day we met. I took his hand and led him out to the car. I strapped him in and prayed to every god I could think of that tonight would go well.

When we walked through the door, everyone was already there. I saw Jaxon and we made our way across the room.

"Hey man. How's it going? No drama yet, right?"

"Naw, man. Not yet. But Solaris just got here. And guess what . . . . . he came stag. I'd keep a close eye on your man." Fucking A. Just my luck.

"Well, that's great. Anyways . . . . Did you bring Piper?"

"Yeah, she's talking to your dad over by the pool."

I never got a chance to introduce Raven to Piper because just then I lost him. I scanned the room rapidly and my eyes fell on him as he was being dragged away by none other than the man I'd been trying to avoid. I ran after them and got in front of Solaris.

"What the hell do you think you're doing?"

"I'm going to play with my new friend." He said innocently but he wasn't fooling me, I could see the lust gleaming in his eyes. I looked back at Raven and had to smile. He was completely confused as to what was going on, but I could tell he wasn't okay with the current situation.

"Um, no you're not. He's mine."

"He can have more than one friend, Oliver. No need to monopolize him. He's a human being, not an item."

"HE may not be an item, but he and I are. He's my boyfriend. And I'm not going to let you do to me what you did to Aphie with Adam. BACK. THE. FUCK. OFF." I snarled at him.

Solaris slowly dropped Raven's hand and backed away. He was moving on but I could see in his eyes that he hadn't given up. I would see him again, and next time he would be there to win.

After that fiasco, it wasn't exactly a secret that Raven and I were dating. All I had to do now was introduced Raven as my boyfriend and pray that everyone liked him. So far so good. I always knew that Raven had a personality that people would like, they just had to get past his sometimes creepy exterior. Today Raven was dressed extremely well, looking more like a rich man's son than a creepy college kid, and he even brought his A-game when it came to impressing my family. I was a little surprised that Jaxon's dad already knew him.

The conversation started with me introducing Raven:

"Hello, Uncle Zander."

"Oliver . . . Well, Jaxon tells me your swim team is undefeated with you on it. That's good. Being the best - that's something to be proud of."

"Yeah, we're pretty fantastic. Anyways, this is Raven Weber. My new boyfriend."

He stood there in silence for a moment. I was lost as to what he was thinking.

Then he clapped me on the shoulder and said, "Good job. Winning the heart of someone . . . now that is something to be proud of. Not to mention, you went the long route and got one that would be difficult. It is needless to say that I am proud of you." As I stood there, slightly shocked at his comment, my mouth hung open slightly and he walked away. Well, I guess that went well.

The night came to a close and followed that pattern the entire night. I introduced Raven, and everyone loved him. I couldn't say that I was surprised, Raven had a sort of light within him that made people like him even though he had a depressing exterior.

The only thing that didn't go the way that I wanted it to is Solaris. I was hoping that my threat would cause him to leave us alone entirely, but life sucks and I have bad luck I guess. Because Solaris spent the entire dinner staring at Raven. Every time someone asked him a question, Solaris hung on every word he said. I had a feeling he wasn't going to just disappear.

15

RAVEN

The dinner went better than I had expected, but now I had to face the same situation with my father. Hopefully, my conversation would receive the same reaction.

We decided it would be better to spend the night at my place. We'd be able to avoid Oliver's father for the night; and since my dad was going to be out late for a meeting with Theodore Hale, my dad's right-hand man, we'd get a little privacy.

We walked into my room and promptly locked the door. I turned to face Oliver and he had loosened his tie and held it in his hand.

He walked up to me and put it around my neck. Then he gently pulled me towards him and kissed me. His lips moved slowly, gentle against mine. They were soft and insistent as they pressed against mine, his need evident. Gradually, the kiss deepened. He moved his head to the side and inserted his tongue into my mouth. Then the kiss became more urgent and aggressive, tasting me in an entirely new way. This is what our first kiss should've been like; sweet and passionate, not filled with lust and aggression. Although don't get me wrong, those were incredible too. But everything Oliver did was incredible.

Slowly, he and I made our way to the foot of the bed and Oliver pushed me down and laid me onto my back, never breaking our kiss.

It was obvious that something was different about this time. It didn't feel rushed or overly aggressive, it was gentle and loving. Every piece of clothing that Oliver removed from me felt like a layer of armor being stripped away revealing my naked body and soul. Every piece of skin that was revealed was then covered with searing kisses, making my body feel as if it was on fire. This was another side of Oliver I had never seen before, but I could get used to it.

Oliver broke our kiss and positioned himself in between my legs. He pushed my legs up to my chest and began licking at my hole. The sensation traveled through me and settled in my, now hard, and pulsing cock. He then eased one finger - and then another - into my hole, now slick with Oliver's saliva. After a few thrusts from his fingers, he removed his fingers leaving me feeling empty inside. A whimper escaped from my slightly parted lips but was quickly replaced by a moan and sigh as Oliver's cock came to rest against my entrance. My breathing hitched and my pulse accelerated as he rocked his hips into me.

Searing pleasure rocked through my body as Oliver's rock hard cock invaded my most sensitive spot. Oliver then began slowly rotating his hips, causing his cock to massage my prostate, sending wave after wave of pleasure through my body.

In the distance, we could hear the front door open and close as my dad came back from his meeting. But Oliver's movements still didn't cease. Instead, he reached up and began jerking me off as he gently rocked into me. A loud moan threatened to escape my mouth, but Oliver pressed his lips to mine and devoured me. I moaned into his mouth and then Oliver bit and roughly sucked my bottom lip. I shivered at the pleasure and felt the familiar tingle in my gut as I came close to my orgasm. I felt myself clench around Oliver's dick.

"Shit, Raven. You're too tight. You're gonna make me come." Oliver panted in my ear.

His words were my undoing and I came hard on his chest as he emptied his seed into my bowels.

We both laid there for what felt like hours, just staring into each other's eyes. Oliver stared back at me with so much love and adoration in his eyes that it made me want to cry. Oliver bent and softly kissed my lips.

We laid there together a second before Oliver pulled me to his side. As I laid my head on Oliver's chest I listened to his heartbeat, perfectly in sync with mine.

"You know something? This is the happiest I've ever been in my life." He said pressing his lips to my head.

I felt my chest tighten and butterflies fill my stomach at his words. "Me too." I breathed in his scent and relaxed into his side.

"I love you," Oliver said those three words. Eight little letters that sent my heart soaring over and over again.

"I love you more."

"That's impossible because I love you the most."

"Well, you know what that means. . ." I said skeptically.

He looked down at me quizzically.

"Means one of us is lying," I said teasingly.

"I would be happy with any amount of love you were willing to give me. As long as you never leave my side."

16

OLIVER

When I woke up the next morning my eyes saw the face of a sleeping angel. Okay, so maybe it wasn't an actual angel. But, God, was he gorgeous. Raven's face was completely expressionless, it was relaxed and peaceful. It felt like a crime to wake him but, as he glanced at his phone, he realized they had slept in. It was around one o'clock in the afternoon, not much longer and Raven's family would be starting the festivities of the day.

Slowly, I wiggled down and out of his grasp and became level with Raven's cock, raised at half-mast thanks to his morning wood. I gripped his shaft and began working my mouth and hand simultaneously up and down his dick. As Raven remained asleep his cock hardened in my mouth. I bobbed my head up and down on his cock until his hand rose and pulled the blanket away from us.

"What are you doing?" He asked sleepily. Apparently his common sense was a little behind in waking up with him because it was extremely obvious what I was doing.

In answer, I swirled my tongue over the tip and then increased the suction once it was completely in my mouth again. My efforts increased as Raven's breathing became shallow. His hand came down and his fingers entangled themselves in my hair as my head bobbed up and down. I reached my hand up and began massaging his balls, rewarding me with a strangled whimper of pleasure from those beautiful pouty lips. His balls tightened in my hand and Raven's salty-sweet cum flowed freely into my mouth. I struggled to swallow it as quickly as he produced it, stray strands trickled down my chin. As I pulled away I licked my lips and captured every last drop of Raven's delicious cum.

Raven pulled me towards him and kissed me deeply.

"That was an awesome wake-up call." He enthused.

I kissed him lightly and said, "I'm glad you liked it. Now it's time to get up." Raven frowned and got out of bed giving me an ever sweet glimpse at his nice ass. But sadly in no time we were both dressed and ready for the day of coming out of the closet. But a deep pit of anxiety still bubbled in my chest.

***

When we walked out of the room Cassie was sitting at the kitchen table eating Lucky Charms. The spoon stopped halfway to her mouth as her eyes landed on me as I walked in behind Raven. Her brow creased in confusion as she tried to make sense of the situation. Then her eyes narrowed in suspicion.

"Hey, where's Dad?" Raven asked nervously.

"He had a meeting with his investors. He said he'd probably be back around two." Cassie announced with confusion still dancing on her features. I watched Raven react to this news and observed him as he visibly relaxed.

"Oh, okay. Well, this is Oliver. Oliver, this is my sister Cassie."

"Yeah, we met when I did an exchange student program last year with Jaxon," I said as I shook her hand.

"Oh, yeah. I remember. You were the guy who had no idea how our school worked. Couldn't speak Italian worth shit either." She described.

"Hey, Jefferson High was completely different from my high school when it comes to rules, we are way more laid back. Not to mention I'm Greek, at least half anyway, and I understand it better than Italian. It just comes naturally."

Cassie was just about to respond when Raven interjected by saying, "Well that's nice. You both know each other. Then today's dinner won't be as bad as I thought it was going to be."

Unfortunately, Cassie chose this time to remember the purpose of the dinner.

"Oh, yeah. I had almost forgotten about dinner. So, Raven, what time is your girlfriend coming?" Both Raven and I flinched at the word 'girlfriend.'

"Um . . . well. We'll just talk about that at dinner time. For now . . . we'll just sit here and talk about anything other than that." Raven stammered.

I watched him for a second and then directed my attention to Cassie.

"So, Cassie, are you and Frank still together?"

Cassie's eyes lit up at the mention of Frank and she launched herself into describing 'thrilling' story after story about her and Frank's blossoming love. It was an extremely dull conversation but I nodded and laughed when appropriate and even threw in some responses of my own, earning a couple of laughs from Cassie and a smoldering look from Raven. Every time Cassie mentioned Frank and their 'serious' relationship I always had a witty response and, when fitting, a couple of innuendos. Cassie was my number one fan after twenty minutes. I've never had an issue with getting people to like me - but when it comes to Raven's family I wanted them to love me, not only as a person, but I also want them to love me for Raven - I wanted them to accept me into their family. Because I know it is important to Raven. After all, he is Italian, and family is everything to him.

***

The day continued without Raven announcing me as his boyfriend to Cassie. I was a little disappointed that he hadn't done it when she had seen us coming out of the room together. I mean, she had been home last night when Raven and I had sex, and even though I had tried to stifle Raven's moans there were still some that managed to slip through our interlocked lips. Cassie was a pretty smart girl, I'm pretty sure she could guess what we were doing behind that locked door. I just hoped that when the dinner started he would actually tell his father that they were dating and not just leave me hanging. I don't know if I could handle it if Raven disrespected me like that.

***

Watching Raven cook: sexiest thing in the world. He would sway his hips to some imaginary music that played inside his head. As he focused on cooking the elaborated Italian meal he bit his lower lip in a way that made me want to capture it in my mouth and suck on it. Everything he did made me horny as hell. The sway of his hips made me want to grab hold of them and fuck him over the stove as he continued cooking. Watching Raven cook: best form of sexual torture.

But now that both Cassie and Raven's dad were home the chances were absolutely none of me fucking Raven any time soon.

"Hey, Raven, I think Oliver's hungry. He keeps staring at you like he's going to jump you and steal the food for himself." Cassie announced observantly. I flinched at her words. It wasn't the food that I wanted to devour, it was Raven.

He turned around slowly and met my gaze. As he took in my expression a blush spread across his cheeks and he went back to cooking.

I stood up and walked to stand behind Raven, acting as if I was trying to see what we were going to have. Then I leaned close to his ear and said, "It's not the food I'm hungry for. But Italian does sound good tonight. How should I prepare for it?"

69

Raven's cheeks flushed a deeper shade of red and replied, "Yeah, Italian does sound good for dinner but for later I'd rather eat some Greek meat. For Italian food, I like to cook the chicken face down and stuff. It gives it a great flavor as it makes its own sauce."

He was testing my will power to not take him in front of his family.

***

In hindsight, it was probably a bad idea for me to spend the night and then spend the entire day at Raven's house waiting for dinner to happen, him to announce our relationship, them to either hate or love me as well as the idea of me fucking their son - as their son's boyfriend, the dinner to end, and then finally get to show some sort of affection towards Raven at my house. It was not only extremely nerve-racking to wait for so long, but I was dying to touch him. But I knew I couldn't touch him until dinner was done, because - when it came to Raven - I was greedy. One touch would lead to me wanting to caress his cheek, a caress would lead to a kiss, and then before you knew it I'd be fucking him on the linoleum.

But I would persevere. And I would get his family to like me.

***

This is the most depressing dinner I have ever attended. It feels like a funeral. Everyone sat around the table wearing black, except for me and Cassie. I wore all black - dress pants, button-up shirt, shoes - except I wore a sea-green tie that matched my eyes. Cassie, on the other hand, wore black leggings and a gold sequence blouse. Her ears were pierced with silver hoop earrings, which the closer I looked at them looked like real silver.

Not only was the dinner boring but I was already pretty sure that Raven's dad didn't like me. Once I met him I extended my hand to shake his and said, "Hello, my name is Oliver Miller. I'm a friend of Raven's." He simply stared at my hand with disgust and asked, "Miller? Why does that name sound familiar? You wouldn't happen to be Fisher Seafarer's son, would you? Of the fishing corporation?" I was slightly surprised by the fact he knew my father and simply nodded but I guess that was the wrong answer because the look of disgust in his eyes only deepened.

In an attempt to create a conversation in the dismal atmosphere I looked at Raven's dad and said, "So, Raven tells me you're in the business of death."

His eyes shifted from Raven to me and said, "You could say that. I basically control everything under the Earth. It has made me a very wealthy man, and has helped provide a comfortable lifestyle for my family."

"Death has made you wealthy? How?"

"Think about it. What is the one thing that will never cease to exist? Death, there is never a shortage of it. Even the mining opportunities will become sparser and sparser as the years go by, but death will always be there."

I nodded my head in understanding, "You have a very interesting view of the world. Slightly depressing, but seemingly accurate."

"Well, what about you? What do you plan on doing with your life, financially wise? You can't hope to live off of your trust fund for the rest of your life."

I laughed softly, "Well, despite what you might think my life is like, due to my father's occupation, you would be incorrect. I have no trust fund. My father has two businesses - the fishing corporation, which will go to my oldest step-brother Tray; and the small military weapon manufacturing company, which is being given to my youngest half-brother Tyson. I am not rich, and I am getting none of my father's businesses. And, just to show you how little of connections I have, Tray hates me and would rather feed himself feet first to a shark before giving me a job at the company. Although Tyson and I are close I am absolutely useless with tools and would probably blow up the plant if he gave me a job. Notice how my last name is Miller and not Seafarer, my father's last name. He tells me I am his favorite son, and I am expected to make my own way through life. I live half the time with my mom and step-father, Paul, in a small apartment in upper Manhattan; the other half is spent at my father's second home where I only see my father three weeks out of a year, which I am using up coming to meet Raven's family. I work in the summer doing whatever job I can land from fast food to dog walking. Using that money, and maybe with some help from my mother, I'll be going to NYU to study marine biology. I have an internship lined up for next summer and I intend to be the absolute best at what I do."

Realizing too late that I probably should've just answered his question and kept my mouth shut I met Raven's father's gaze without fear. After several minutes there was a slight twinkle in his eyes and he smiled and nodded his head.

"Anyways," said Cassie trying to break the tension. "When is your girlfriend getting here, Raven? She's like twenty minutes late."

"Um . . . about that. I don't have a girlfriend." Raven said nervously.

"So . . . She's not coming?"

"No, I just don't have a girlfriend," he explained firmly.

"Did you guys break up?"

"No, I just don't have a girlfriend," Raven repeated.

"So you lied about her coming to dinner."

"Yes and no."

"Because you guys broke up before the dinner."

"No, I made her up. She never existed. I don't have a girlfriend, I never did."

"Wait - what? I'm confused. Then why did you have a used condom?"

I coughed and choked on the food I was eating and Raven's parents stopped eating completely, his stepmother completely pushing her plate away in distaste.

Raven rubbed his temples roughly and said, "I told you it wasn't mine. And I never threw a party, so it must've been yours."

Cassie blushed and said softly, "I don't think we've ever done it in the kitchen."

I pushed my food away from me. I looked at Raven pointedly and he nodded.

"Cassie, I am one hundred percent sure that I don't have, nor have I ever had, a girlfriend. And I will never have a relationship with a female because I am one hundred percent gay." Raven explained calmly but with a flicker of irritation in his voice.

"Now that makes more sense!" Exclaimed Raven's step-mom.

I laughed out loud and then quickly regained my calm expression.

Mrs. Weber looked at Raven's dad and said, "I told you it was fake. Everything about him screams gay. He has style, he's frail, not to mention his extremely feminine butt." Then she looked at Raven and said, "Don't get me wrong, I don't mind your gayness. And, just like the last conversation that was shared, it's none of my business either way. I've always been a bit of a flower child like that; the whole love whoever thing and all."

Raven's dad nodded and said, "To be honest, son, I was a little skeptical as well. You've never talked about any girls you liked and was always extremely secretive when it came to your love life and where you spent the night some days. Although, I will say that I am disappointed that you felt the need to hide it when asked about it."

"Well, I wasn't necessarily hiding it. I just wasn't ready to talk about it yet."

He nodded again. "Understandable. Now, I am assuming that you, Mr. Miller, are the one that is in a relationship with my son?"

"Yes, sir. you would be correct. I took him to meet all of my family yesterday. They loved him almost as much as I do. My cousin, Solaris, might've loved him a little more than I'd have liked but other than that it went over quite well with my entire family." I smiled fondly at Raven and placed my hand on his thigh, finally feeling the connection I've been craving all day.

"Wonderful. I hope one of these days in the future we could all get together," said Mrs. Weber.

I nodded and glanced at Cassie. Her face was white and confusion was the only thing I could see in her feature.

"Cassie, what's wrong?" I asked.

"Okay, so, homosexuality. It's sort of normal here right?"

"Yes, fairly."

"Okay, then which one of you is on the bottom?" She asked as if it was an obvious question that needed to be answered.

"Um...-" I stammered. It was the last thing I had expected her to ask.

"I am." Announced Raven, unashamed.

"Oh, okay. that makes sense. Okay, now I'm better."

Even though the conversation was over I still had a faint blush lingering on my cheeks. Cassie had surprised me. When I thought about the dinner I had expected questions about our future and either approval or disapproval. I was not expecting to have our sex life inquired upon.

***

As the night came to a close Raven and I prepared to go back to my place. It had been an exceedingly long day and I deserved a few days of drama-free life filled with never-ending sex, at least on the weekends anyway. The best part of that is it's Christmas break, so there was plenty of time for us.

17

RAVEN

Since the day of my 'coming out' dinner, Oliver and I have admittedly become much happier. Just the fact that we weren't a secret anymore made our lives that much easier.

It is now Christmas Eve and sadly, on this snowy morning, I woke up alone in Oliver's queen size bed. Beside me, there was a note indication to Oliver's whereabouts but the empty feeling was still there. I slowly got out of bed, careful not to move too quickly due to the soreness of having phenomenal sex with Oliver almost every night, and made my way to the bathroom for a much-needed shower. I felt all of the sweat and fatigue from our nightly 'exercise' fall off of me as the hot water flowed over my pale skin.

Once I was done washing I wrapped a towel around my waist and stepped out of the bathroom. I heard the door open and shut as Oliver returned home and I went to welcome him while in my towel-clad body.

"Hey, welcome home -" My voice fell short as I came face to face with someone who wasn't Oliver.

His golden eyes trailed hungrily down my body as he noticed my near nakedness. When he stepped towards me I took a cautious step back.

"Hey, Raven. What're you doing here?" He asked as he continued assessing my appearance.

"Solaris. I'm waiting for Oliver. He said we were gonna spend the day together. I just got out of the shower." I explained.

"Merry Christmas to Oliver then." He said his eyes were still feasting on my scantily-clad body. Having Solaris' eyes watch me in a way I would only want Oliver to was quickly making me uncomfortable. I raised my hands and attempted to cover my body, unsuccessfully due to my thin arms and small hands.

"Um . . . yeah, I guess. Look, I'm gonna go get dressed. If you're waiting for Oliver, I don't know what time he'll be back but of course, you are welcome to stay and wait for him." I said anxiously as I tried desperately to get out of this exceedingly awkward situation. But quicker than I had thought possible, Solaris was blocking my path to the bedroom and said, "But that would be such a waste. I think you look good, very natural," while licking his lips.

"Thanks, I guess. But no . . . I'm gonna get dressed. Oliver gets extremely jealous and I would hate for him to get the wrong idea." I tried to make another move towards the bedroom but again Solaris blocked my path.

"And what impression is that?" Solaris asked with fake innocence.

"That anything is going on between us," I said plainly.

"Oh, but isn't there? I'm feeling quite an intense attraction to you, Raven. I'm sure you can feel it too." He said, taking another step towards me.

Quickly, I took another step back and said, "No, no attraction. Just extreme awkwardness. I'd like for you to keep your attraction, and other parts of your body, to yourself, please."

Faster than a panther, Solaris pounced. Sending both of us tumbling to the floor as he held my wrists above my head and straddled my hips.

"Now, Raven, what are you feeling?" He whispered into my ear as he moved to yank my towel away.

"Fear. Lots of fear. Still that awkwardness. And yeah . . . your dick against my hip."

Solaris didn't even seem to register my words as he started to undo his pants to pull out his hard cock.

He laid his cock in front of him and said, "Now how does that look?"

"Small," was the only word that came out of my mouth.

The look of rage on Solaris' face was quite amusing. I don't think anyone has ever told him that he had a small penis before. But what do you expect? Oliver's dick was at least an inch thicker and maybe two inches longer than his. But of course, no man ever wants to hear that, I mean I'm the bottom in Oliver and my relationship and I'm still pretty sure I'd kick him in his dick if he called my dick small, and Solaris definitely didn't want to hear that. He raised his hand to slap me in the face.

Luckily that was the exact moment Oliver walked through the front door. And I'm sure you could imagine that the glare Oliver gave Solaris could have rivaled Medusa's.

Solaris never got the chance to react to Oliver's entrance because he might not have been frozen in stone, but he sure as hell was frozen in fear. Then Oliver was on him.

He pulled Solaris off of me and proceeded to beat the shit out of him. I didn't even move to stop him. I mean, for all I knew Solaris had intended to rape me. Only Oliver was allowed to touch me in those intimate places, forcefully or otherwise.

Once Solaris' face began to look like ground hamburger meat, I pulled Oliver off of him. I wasn't about to let Oliver become responsible for killing his cousin, even if he did deserve it. He didn't get farther than embarrassing himself, so there was no harm done. But if Oliver hadn't shown up I shudder to think what could have happened.

Oliver grabbed Solaris and threw him out the front door and into the lawn, he spat on him and then yelled, "I'm calling your family and telling them what you did. That way I won't need to kill you, your dad will do it for me!" Then he slammed the door, hugged me, and buried his face in my neck whispering apologies the entire time. I just stood there, rubbed his back, and whispered back that I was fine and that it was okay.

***

That night we went to Oliver's mom's house for dinner. I love his mom. Everyone does. She's so nice and calm that it's hard not to like her. Not to mention the millions of baby stories of Oliver being in the bathtub, of course with pictures to go with them. But to be honest, I much preferred the idea of the current Oliver naked in a bathtub. But I'll stick a pin in that for later tonight.

Once dinner was over Oliver and I cleared the table together and washed the dishes. Every time he and I were alone he would grope my ass, pull me into an embrace, or even kiss me so hard I saw stars. I didn't mind it as long as his parents were in a different room though.

As I leaned my head against Oliver's shoulder I remembered how I didn't care for Christmas. It had never been a big holiday in my family, we were more suited for the solstice and Halloween. But I knew Oliver loved it. But I couldn't think of anything to get him. He never told me what he wanted either. I tried not to focus on the present I was preparing to give him on Christmas night, because I wouldn't be able to stand and tell his parents goodnight if I did.

18

OLIVER

I'm laying in bed, staring at the ceiling, just wondering how I ever got so lucky. I feel the tingle of Raven's breath on my chest and it calms me. We are almost always together now, and I wouldn't change it for all the money in the world.

My phone dings as I receive a text message, it's Tyson.

Tyson: Brother!!! I'm almost there for Christmas!!! Don't open presents without me, I'm a block away!

Me: Don't worry dude we aren't even out of bed yet you're good.

Fuck yeah, he's almost here!

My brother Tyson is the best guy ever I swear. People tend to think he's slow and dangerous because he doesn't seem smart and he's huge, but he's great with his hands and he jacked. Underneath it all though he's just a big softy. I can understand why people steer clear though; he lost an eye in an accident when he was a kid and just never felt the need to get a glass one or anything just slapped an eye patch on and called it a day, he was already over six feet tall when I was first introduced to him by my dad and that was when we were in seventh grade, he's jacked as fuck from working for my dad at his weapons manufactory so he looks like a monster. However, his girlfriend Ella can attest that Tyson is one of the sweetest guys you'll ever meet. Everyone that gets to know him ends up loving him.

I hear pounding on the door as I quietly slip my pants on. I hurry to the front door holding my pants up, just trying to let them in before he wakes everyone up.

I open the door to a grinning Tyson and a shy Ella who has started to blush as she notices my disheveled appearance. Tyson, completely oblivious, drags both of their suitcases in and wraps me in a tight bear hug.

"Tyson . . . . . I . . . . can't . . . breathe!" I gasp. He lets go and I quickly scramble to catch my pants as I land heavily on the ground.

"Brother . . . your clothes. They look different than normal." He says confusedly as he notices my rumpled clothes, and lack thereof.

"Yeah well, you caught me at a bad time." I laugh. "I'm gonna go get dressed, okay? Everyone should be awake soon."

I hurry to the bedroom to get dressed, as I go to slip my shirt down over my naked chest I feel a slim hand run up my abs and wrap around my waist.

"What do you think you're doing?" Raven says lustfully as tries to pull my shirt back over my head.

"My brother's here with his girlfriend. You need to get dressed too, everyone is gonna be getting up to eat breakfast and open presents." I explain as I tug my shirt out of his greedy hands.

Raven pouts and releases me from his grasp. I sigh as I watch this adorableness unfold. His full bottom lip pouts and he crosses his arms over his chest. Fucking adorable. The only thing out of place was his slim frame only covered by my t-shirt maybe two sizes too big for his figure. I have never seen him as tempting as he is now with his hair tousled and looking like sex on legs. What I would give to sink hilt deep in that milky white ass, but we had people waiting. And knowing Tyson, if I took too long he would just barge it, with my luck while I was mid-fuck.

I tossed Raven's skinny jeans in his face and the pout intensified. I couldn't help but smile.

"You're adorable, you know that right?" I say as I give him a peck on his lips. He snakes his hands around my neck and deepens the kiss, my resolve starting to crumble as Raven's will overpowered mine. My sex-drive spiked and I started to devour Raven's lips. I climbed on top of him, continuing the kiss and groping his ass. My hand kneaded the bare flesh as I felt his hand roaming all over my body. His hands made their way back to my neck and his fingers laced into my hair. He gives a slight pull and I moan against his lips. My tongue and his entwined as reason tried to fight its way back to the surface but my lust is a tough opponent. I break our kiss and attack Raven's tender flesh at his neck, he pulls on my hair again a little harder and I growl. I pin Raven to the bed with his hands above his head and go back to attacking the incubus laying underneath me.

There's a knock at the door but I ignore it as I focus all my attention on the delicious meal before me. I suck Raven's bottom lip into my mouth and nip at it before I deepen the kiss as my veins throb and my heart explodes. I have never wanted anyone like this before. The most delicious smell I could ever imagine was coming from him, it made me want to breathe him, lick him, eat him, drink him. His lips taste like honey. I couldn't stop. the world melted around me and all I could see, hear, feel was Raven.

Until the spell was shattered by Tyson bursting in "Brother everyone's awake . . . " and stopping mid-sentence as he saw the erotic scene before him. Luckily my body covered Raven's completely as we both jolt and look towards the doorway.

"Hey . . . . Tyson . . . . can you give me a second?" I laugh nervously. Hell of a way for him to find out about Raven and me, I mean everyone else knew but I had yet to tell him.

He shuts the doors slowly peering in through the still present opening until it fully closes.

"And that was why I was getting dressed." I hiss at Raven as I throw his clothes back in his face. I'm not mad, a little embarrassed, but not mad. "Come on, you should get dressed before he comes back." I laugh.

19

RAVEN

I'm positive this is my fault when it comes down to it, but I honestly wasn't thinking. My mind just blanks sometimes with Oliver, like I become a different person. I can't help it that I just want my hands on him every moment of every day. And with both of us out of the closet, well, for the most part, I wasn't exactly afraid of getting caught anymore.

The scene in front of us was hilarious, to say the least. Tyson was sitting with a perplexed expression on his face, Ella had turned bright red from embarrassment, Mom was stirring batter for pancakes as Paul pulled a batch of cookies out of the oven while whistling Christmas music. Oliver was sitting hunched over on the couch with his elbows on his knees and his hands dangling between his knees. Luckily I wasn't dumb enough to laugh. It was obvious that Oliver didn't want Tyson to find out like that.

"Tyson, buddy, so . . . . That's not exactly how I wanted you to find out about Raven and me." Oliver says as I rub his back with my hand as he spoke.

"Brother . . . . . You should lock the door next time. So are you and Death Boy like me and Ella now?"

"Don't call him that, Tyson. His name's Raven. But yeah, we are dating." Oliver says, finally meeting Tyson's eyes.

"Smells like depression." Says Tyson matter of factly.

"Tyson," Sally warns curtly as she flips a pancake in the kitchen. The warning from that one word was enough to get an apology from Tyson.

"But what about Anna?"

"We haven't been together in forever, Tyson. She got too busy after she got that architectural internship. We just didn't have time for each other anymore and grew apart."

Tyson sighs, "I liked Anna."

"Tyson," Sally warns again, earning another apology from Tyson.

Tyson looks Oliver in the eye and says, "Brother . . . . are you happy?"

He gives his usual smile and says, "Yeah. I am. I'm honestly the happiest I've ever been." He grabs my hand and brings it to his lips. "I love him."

"Then I will be happy too. As long as Raven will make my brother happy." Tyson nods at his statement satisfied.

Paul claps his hands together in the kitchen and says, "Great! Breakfast is served!"

OLIVER

Everyone gathered around the Christmas tree and started to hang out presents. There was a knock at the door and Mom got up to answer it.

"Hey Oliver, look who's here." She called from the other room. I turn towards the door to see my dad leaning against the door frame with of course a floral print Hawaiian shirt and Bermuda shorts on . . . . in December. Only he could stand that kind of cold. But I guess everyone knows at least one person who wears shorts in the winter.

"Hey, Dad! You aren't with the step-monster for Christmas?"

Dad frowns and says, "You know I don't like you referring to her like that. I know you don't get along with Amy but you need to at least put forth the effort."

I scoff, "You're joking, right? Amy, Tray, and Kym have hated me before I had even met them. They are dicks. The only one who I haven't had issues with is Ronnie and let's be honest it's because we've never been left in the same room alone together and I'd like to keep it that way."

"I thought you and Kym were on good terms. What happened?"

"She tried to drown me in the pool, Dad! I mean, yeah, we are better NOW after Jaxon convinced her to let me fucking breathe, but seriously! She's a fucking psycho!"

"Yeah, we are looking at counseling for her right now. I had completely forgotten about that little incident. Anyway!" He said with a clap of his hands. "I knew you were probably gonna stay with your mom for a bit so I figured I'd bring everyone's presents here."

Dad pulls out a bunch of boxes and takes a seat on the couch, making himself comfortable. Everyone begins opening their presents and yelling in excitement for whatever they got.

Tyson got a new hammer set for work, which he was very excited about. Mom got a pearl necklace from my dad, she tried to give it back but Dad refused and Paul told her it would be rude to refuse his gift so she agreed to accept it in the end. Ella got a book, which was memorized in like four seconds.

Raven was given a new leather jacket and then it was my turn.

"I'm not proposing or anything so don't get any crazy ideas," I say as I hand him a small box. Raven opens it to reveal a skull ring but rather than being black or silver, it's blue. The exact shade of my eyes.

"Not gonna lie, the color will definitely stand out against the rest of my wardrobe." Raven laughs. "But I love it."

"Sooooooo?" I ask expectantly. "Where's mine?" I bat my eyelashes.

"Well now I feel bad," Raven laughs. "Mine wasn't romantic like yours. I went for something fun." He pulls my present out from under the tree and hands it over. I unwrap it and a child-like grin spreads across my face.

"You got me *Final Fantasy VII?*" A new video game that had come out two days ago, right in time for Christmas, I had been wanting to get it but I just hadn't had the time to go pick it up.

Dad begins to stand and walks over to us and says, "Hey, son, so I'm about to head out now I just wanted to go ahead and give you your present before I left." He hands me a pamphlet and I stare questioningly at it for a moment. I opened it and read the letters.

"You got me a vacation to Montauk?" I ask, amazed.

"Actually, I bought that cabin I used to take your mom to back in the day. As I understand you and her used to take vacations there often when you were in middle school. So it's in your name. You guys can go whenever you want. I had it refurbished and I figured you and Raven could take a trip during the break or something." He says smiling.

I wrap him in a tight hug and say, "It's amazing, Dad. I love it. We will definitely be using this often."

Dad gives me a tight hug before he heads to the door and stops, "Oh! I almost forgot! Paul! I got you something too!"

He hands him a heavy present which Paul opens revealing a worn leather-bound book. "*Pericles, Prince of Tyre?* 1609!? This is the first edition?"

"Yeah! A little guppy told me you used to do a little Shakespeare in college. This is the least I can do for you taking care of Sally and Oliver these past few years. Even though Sally and I aren't together anymore I still want the best for her and of course, Oliver deserves a break in life. I'm happy they have you in their life."

Paul just stood there staring at the old book and then just sat heavily on the couch. "Thank you." He whispers astounded.

"Alright, I'm heading out. Merry Christmas everyone!"

My mom stands up after everyone has finished opening presents and says, "So before everyone continues their other holiday plans me and Paul have an announcement!" I look around at everyone just watching intently as she says, "I'm pregnant! We are expecting a baby girl in March!"

I gasp and smile excitedly. "I'm gonna have a little sister?!"

20

RAVEN

We arrived at Montauk beach just before seven pm on Christmas day, both of us not wanting to spend the holiday evening apart after that kiss that was interrupted this morning. Oliver grabbed both of our overnight bags in one go and tossed me over his shoulder as he ran inside.

"You realize I can walk right?!" I yell down at him as he runs for the door.

"You mean the depressing little foot shuffle that you do? No way in hell. I'm not waiting that long to have my way with you without a possibility of interruption. I've been thinking of what other Christmas present you could give me tonight all fucking day and I'm so ready it hurts." He closes the threshold and throws our bags in the corner of the room and rushes into the bedroom.

Where he very unceremoniously tosses me onto the bed and begins stripping off his clothes and then moving onto mine.

OLIVER

All of my patience is gone as I devour Raven's lips. I moaned as I felt his tongue dart across my lips, then he pulled away and looked into my eyes. Raven moved back in and kissed me harder, I pushed him flat against the bed. I climbed on top of him, and I lost track of time as our tongues probed each other. I could feel his bare thighs against mine, our hard cocks grinding and pressing together, his chest pressing against me, and our mouths locked together. Raven rolls on top of me, taking control and locks our lips back together. I ran my hands down his back and grabbed his ass, my fingers reaching into his crack. He started kissing my neck, then trailed his tongue down my chest, stopping just before reaching my cock.

Raven smiled as he wrapped his tongue around my cock head. I let out a moan as his lips moved down my shaft, his hot wet mouth engulfing me. I ran my fingers into his hair as his head started moving slowly up and down. I focused on his movements and the feeling of his tongue swirling around the head of my cock, almost bringing myself close to orgasm. Just then, he stopped, looked up, and smiled. He leaned over me to reach for something out of his bag in the corner. He came back with a tube of lubricant in his hand. He opened it up and reached down between his legs to grease up my cock; then he poured some on his fingers and reached back to finger his hole, the lube dripped down his thighs. When he moved back, his balls were dangling in front of my cock and he leaned back a little. My dickhead pressed up against his hole until it popped through. He slowly sat back onto me, his ass gripping ever tighter and further down my shaft. Such intense heat. He pulled back up slowly and I thought I would pass out. The feeling of his hot ass sliding up my shaft was almost too much. He leaned down and covered my mouth with his as he started bobbing up and down on my cock. He sat back up again and started moving faster and faster. We both started to moan as he covered my mouth again, our tongues moving back and forth while his ass kept bouncing up and down. Suddenly he let out a grunt with his lips still pressed against mine. I felt a hot splash against my neck as his shot squirted out of his cock. His grunts got louder and louder as each squirt covered my chest and stomach until finally, I couldn't hold back. He sat down on my crotch as I fired shot after shot of cum up inside his ass. I looked down to see his balls resting on my pubic area and my body shook with each pulse out of my dick. He carefully got off of me and collapsed onto my chest.

"That was amazing. but I'm not done yet." I growl before I pull Raven back up to my lips. We crash together again without a care in the world, knowing that we had the whole place to ourselves until the first. Raven's hands roamed my body hungrily as I caressed his sides and tweaked his nipples. God, I loved how expressive he was. Every touch of mine was rewarded by every sigh and moan that escaped those beautiful lips of his. I bit down on his neck and nibbled as the sensitive flesh. Leaving a mark that I'm sure he will be mad about in the morning. But right now he was all mine.

I position myself over him and trail my way down to his quivering member, as I slide my lips around it slowly I suck and lick at the semi hardness until he is fully erect. His last orgasm was still present on the tip of his cock; I slurp and lick at the salty taste. The taste of my lovely Raven. I pull away and insert two fingers into his leaking ass and pump into him earning some wanton gasps and moans from Raven as my finger feels the fullness of my last orgasm inside him.

"I love how your tight little ass is so full of my cum." I say licking my lips. Raven's arms go up to cover his face as it turns red.

"Don't talk about it!" He exclaims with embarrassment.

I pull my fingers out and slowly insert myself into his more than ready entrance. Ready to fill him with my cum all over again. I reach up and pull Raven's arms from his face holding them above his head.

"Now why are you hiding from me? I want you to watch as I fuck you. I want you to watch my cock pound your ass as it leaks my cum." Raven pulls his arms from my grasp and wraps them around my neck pulling my mouth to his. He bites at my lip and then slips his tongue into my mouth. Passion erupts inside me and I am no longer fucking. Our bodies move and grind together as we make love fervently. I slowly push my cock in and out of him.

"I love you." Raven moans.

"I love you too," I say as I lock our lips together once again. I grab Raven by the waist and pull him to me in tandem as I thrust into him making each thrust feel that much deeper.

"Mmmmmmm. Oliver, I'm gonna cum. Raven says as he looks in my eyes.

"Do it, baby. I'm gonna come too." Raven cums as I thrust deep inside of him releasing my orgasm and depositing my cum inside him with each thrust. I pull out and smile down at him.

"Now THAT was fantastic."

Raven grins back. "It was. But now I need a shower; because I am disgusting." He hops up out of bed and I smack his ass quickly.

"Hurry back," I say with the biggest grin on my face.

21

RAVEN

I wake to the sunbeams cascading in from the window as the morning sun peeked over the lake outside. I stretch and go to get out of bed, but a pair of strong arms wrap around my waist and pull me into the little spoon position.

"Now where do you think you're going?" Asks Oliver tiredly. How does he sound so damn sexy first thing in the morning?

"Well, I was gonna go get something to eat. But I guess not anymore." I say turning around in his arms to face him.

"Uh-huh. You're not going anywhere." He says as he rubs his nose against mine and kisses my lips softly.

"You're lucky I want to stay in bed with you, otherwise I could get out of this," I say with a mock threat in my tone.

"Oh yeah? You think so?" A half-smile playing across those beautiful lips of his.

I wiggle slightly. "Oh yeah, definitely. This hold? Easily." I attempt to wiggle out and he's on top of me in an instant, both of my slim wrists held in one of his large hands over my head.

"Still think you can get out?"

"Yeah just gimme a sec," I say as I wiggle my hips underneath him and stain my arms in an attempt to get free. My brow crinkling in frustration.

"I don't think so, Mister." Then he begins to tickle my sides with his free hand. I thrash about laughing.

"Ha ah! Oliver, stop! That tickles!" I scream in between bouts of laughter. His fingers become more relentless as he moves to my armpits and then down to my stomach. I buck my hips underneath him as I struggle to get free.

"Ahhhh, Oliver! Please!" I laugh loudly. Oliver's onslaught comes to a stop and then he leans in and kisses me, releasing my hands.

I pull away from the kiss and look deep into his eyes, "Wanna go swimming?" I ask excitedly.

The look of disappointment was obvious on his face as he nodded slowly and got off of me. I run to the bathroom with my swim trunks and slip them on. Coming out of the bathroom, Oliver's eyes scanning my half-naked body hungrily, I notice his choice of swimsuit.

"Aww, I was kind of hoping you'd choose the swim team speedo," I said disappointed.

Oliver laughs and says, "I mean I have my swim bag in the car if you want me to change."

I shrug and say, "Don't worry about it, you're already in this one. Buuuuuuut let's remember that when we are in bed later. You have no idea how often I use to jerk off to the thought of you in next to nothing during swim meets." I blush at the memory.

"You better get that sexy ass in that water before I change my mind about letting you out of this room." Oliver threatens with dark eyes.

I blanch and take off with him close behind me, obviously letting me get a bit of a lead. I dive into the water and sweep back my wet hair as I break the surface, Oliver nowhere in sight. I looked around confused and then I was pulled underwater. Oliver's arms wrapped around me underwater and his lips were on me as we broke the surface. I was breathing hard against his mouth but I didn't care. We were ferocious in our movements as Oliver's fingers were inside my ass, penetrating me as the Montauk water cooled my skin in its feverish state. I wrapped my legs around his waist and he slowly inserted himself inside me as I moaned against his lips. Oliver being as tall as he is standing in the water with it up to his chest thrusts inside me as he holds my legs around his waist.

"Fuck it's cold." He says as he pounds into me the water splashing around us.

"Why did I want to swim again?" I say not shivering yet as the friction heats me.

"Because you're fucking crazy." He says thrusting deeper, he grasps my cock and jerks me off to push my orgasm along.

Oliver and I grunt and cum together. Oliver breathes heavily and pulls out of me. He rests his forehead on mine and he just holds me for a moment as someone down the beach at another cabin yells over, "You know you aren't supposed to swim here right?"

Oliver and I laugh as we swim to the shore. "Aren't you boys cold?" He shouts out at us.

"Freezing!" I yell over with smiles on both of our lips.

"No shit kid it's fucking December!" He yells back. We run inside shivering as we hear him grumbling about dumb ass kids.

22

OLIVER

The next morning entering the school had me in a panic. There were flyers everywhere with me pressing Raven up against the wall. From the looks of it it had been taken while we were in Montauk. I have no idea who would have seen us there, it would have had to have been someone from school, obviously, someone who recognized us immediately. Although, to someone who wasn't there, the picture on the flyers didn't make it obvious what we were doing and you couldn't tell it was even Raven in the picture. But right next to the picture of our hot encounter was a blown-up picture of Raven's hand where there was a skull ring, one that matched the color of my eyes.

Everyone was staring at me as I frantically searched for my 'Mystery woman' but then I stopped. If I went and found Raven in this state the cat would be out of the bag.

I pulled out my phone and texted Raven: *Take off your skull ring now. They are looking for it*

"I guess it's good I'm not at school yet then" Raven texts back. I breathe a sigh of relief.

"Are you running late?"

"Yeah. Cassie hasn't done laundry recently so I didn't have my usual stuff to wear. So don't cum in your pants when you see me. This is all I had." I read the final text right as I turn towards the front entrance and watch as a sexy Italian walks in and, like always, steals my heart.

Raven was HOT. He was wearing a black pair of slim-fitting black jeans with rips from the upper thigh down to his shin. So. Much. Skin. A v-neck t-shirt that showed just enough definition of his lean body was worn under a zip-up hoodie underneath a leather jacket. A beanie was on his head wrangling his always messy hair into a very sexy look. My guess? Bedhead. Probably woke up ten minutes ago. On his feet, he wore some black converse, pretty much the only thing I had ever seen him in before today. And never has a secret relationship been so painful up until now. All I wanted to do was touch him, maybe whisper how sexy he looked in his ear.

Raven noticed me drooling down the hallway and waved as he walked towards me. "Goddammit, Weber. How am I supposed to keep my hands to myself when you come here looking like that?" I say discreetly.

"What? Did you expect me to leave any part of this outfit off just to make you less horny? Not gonna happen." My eyes roamed greedily down his body and rested on his hand, now absent of the ring I had given him.

"You're not wearing the ring. Good."

"Well, I wouldn't say *that*," Raven says as he tugs at a silver chair that's tucked into his shirt. I smile. Even though not wearing the ring is for his own good I'm secretly glad that he still found a way to wear it anyway.

The bell rings and we make our way to our separate classes.

RAVEN

The jingle of my chain on my neck as I walk to class gives me slight comfort as I notice how light my hand feels without the ring on it. It gives me a sense of anxiety just knowing it isn't on my finger. But the coolness of the metal calms me down every time. He's still here with me.

I enter my class and every pair of eyes in the room turns and stares at me. I hear whispers from every girl in the room. *Is that Raven? What happened? I can't believe he's actually hot. Do you think he has a girlfriend?*

I mentally roll my eyes as I listen to their annoying gossiping. I collapse into my chair and rest my head on my desk. Today was gonna be a long day.

"Ahem." I hear to my left. I look up to see a girl probably about five foot three with red-dyed hair, a beanie on her head, black-rimmed glasses pushed up on the brim on her nose, and a white v-neck t-shirt with the front tucked into her short jean shorts with tights underneath and combat boots on her feet. I have no idea who she is.

"Can I help you?" I ask tiredly.

"It's Raven, right?" She asks with her arms behind her back and her chest noticeably pushed out. If I was playing for the right team I'm sure her posture would be irresistible. Unlucky for her she was probably gonna regret coming over here this morning. God, I'm tired. I didn't sleep at all last night until two hours before my alarm clock went off because I was too busy worrying about Alyssa and her goons, I overslept, didn't get my morning coffee, and I felt extremely out of place in my current wardrobe.

"That would be me."

Her finger begins to twirl in her hair and she bites her bottom lip. Okay, I see what's happening now. "Um well, I was wanting to know if you would want to go out with me this weekend?" She leans down now resting her elbows on my desk bringing her face dangerously close to mine. I notice as she gives a slight arch in her back, making her ass more noticeable. This poor girl. Her ego's gonna hurt after this one.

Her friends could be heard giggling from the back corner of the room as they watch us not so discreetly.

"No thanks," I say bluntly and push her elbows off my desk. Her face is full of shock as I begin plugging my headphones in and put one then the other into my ears.

I feel her pull my left earbud out and I sigh, "What?"

"I'm a little confused. I was asking you out. This is the part where you say sorry and say you'll pick me up at eight." She says as if I don't understand plain English.

"Yeah, no, I understood. No, thanks." And stuck the headphone back in. No music was playing yet so I could plainly hear the smattering of gasps and laughter from around the classroom.

My earphone was pulled out again this time more violently. I huff out a breath and turn my body towards her with my elbows on my knees, hands clasped in between my knees. "What?" I said getting more irritated now.

"Why?" She asks with fire dancing in her vibrant green eyes.

"First of all, you don't know anything about me. Secondly, I don't even know what your name is and, frankly, I don't care. Thirdly, I'm in a relationship. And lastly, because you seem extremely full of yourself." I'm very grouchy when I don't get my morning coffee and this bitch was not making it easy to be nice to her.

She pushes me back in my chair and straddles me, wrapping her arm around my neck. "My name's Selena. And your girlfriend doesn't have to know. Come on, I know you want me." She said as she brought her lips closer to mine.

I push her off my lap abruptly and say, "Well, Selena my answer remains the same. No and no."

She glares at me from the floor and growls. Because that'll make you more attractive.

"I will have you. No punk freak turned hunk is gonna turn me down." She says as she stands back up.

"Good luck seducing a gay man, Selena. I wish you all the luck." I say as I once again put my earbuds in and turn my music on, faintly hearing a screech coming from Selena. Very ladylike. I shake my head. God, I miss my hoodies.

23

RAVEN

Selena was following me. Every time I stopped in the hallway she'd be there to lean against the wall next to me when I stopped at my locker she'd be there when I shut the door. I hadn't seen Oliver yet but I'm sure he wouldn't like my new-found shadow.

The lunch bell rang and I made my way to my usual table where Oliver was already waiting for me. I sat down and heard the chair next to me scrape against the tile as my shadow took a seat next to me.

I sighed in irritation as Oliver's confused gaze went from me to her. "Don't fucking ask," I say as he begins to open his mouth. More than likely to ask what the fuck is going on.

Selena popped her gum and held her hand out to shake Oliver's hand as she said, "Hi, Raven and I just started going out. My name's Selena." Oliver's eyebrows shot up and then abruptly narrowed as he completely ignored her hand. His eyes bore into my soul as he awaited my explanation.

"No the hell we aren't, Selena. I've told you around seven times today I wasn't fucking interested and that I was already seeing someone. So kindly. Fuck. Off." I said through clenched teeth, my anger getting the better of me. This arrogant bitch couldn't take a well-spelled out hint, could she?

"And I told you I didn't give a fuck. They don't have to know. I'm not letting you get away after I found out what potential you really have."

"I don't see why my 'potential' has anything to do with this. Come Monday I'll be right back in my hoodies and oversized t-shirts. It'll be like this," I reasoned gesturing to my outfit, "never happened."

"Well, obviously you will need to put in more effort while dating me. I mean, I can't have you walking around looking like emo-gone-wrong on my watch."

Oliver was struggling to keep his cool as she continued to stake her undeserved and unwanted claim on me. I signaled him with my eyes not to worry, I could handle this.

"Selena, did you miss the part where I said I was gay? I have absolutely no interest in you and there is nothing that you can do to change that fact. You have no effect on me and, honestly, your personality leaves a lot to be desired too."

"Bullshit. I know you only said you were gay to get me to give up. It's not going to work. I don't care if I have to fuck you right here to prove it." Selena was getting angry now; rising from her chair to get in my face.

I stood up slowly, looked her in the eye, and said, "I don't care if you do a fucking strip tease right now, the fucking janitor has a better chance of getting my dick hard than you do."

Her face turned a dark scarlet as her anger and embarrassment at my words became overwhelming. That's when she punched me. My face felt like I had been hit by an aluminum bat rather than a sixteen-year-olds fist. I held my cheek and flexed my jaw, her angry glare still on me. Then her eyes locked on something else. Something on my chest.

I looked down to see my chain with my ring on it laying on my chest, no longer tucked into my shirt. The force of me hitting the ground must have caused it to fall out. People were gathering around now as they came to witness the aftermath of Selena and my fight. Including the girl I saw with Alyssa the day she put a hit out on me. She immediately zeroed in on the ring and quickly pulled out her phone and took a picture of me on the ground.

Selena's eyes were slowly connecting the dots as Oliver helped me off the ground and checked my face for what would probably lead to a nasty bruise tomorrow morning. Her eyes darted from me to Oliver and everything fell into place.

"Fuck," Oliver whispered as a commotion from the cafeteria doors started and Alyssa came busting into the circle of people that had surrounded us. Her eyes landed on me and then went to the ring dangling on the chain around my neck.

"So this is why you never said yes any of the times I asked you out," Alyssa said in realization.

Oliver stepped in front of me in a protective stance and said, "Alyssa, I don't know what to tell you at this point. Even when I was dating girls I wasn't interested. I think it's your personality. You're just toxic. And the fact that you put out a hit on someone I love just because I told you no doesn't help your situation."

Alyssa's eyes dilated at the L-word. "You actually love this gross kid?" Her words laced with distaste.

"No, no, no, no, no!" Screamed Selena, her foot stamping as she threw her temper tantrum. "He's mine! You can't have him."

With the cat out of the bag there was nothing holding Oliver back at this point, he snapped. "No! He's mine! His lips, his ass, his heart, and soul are all mine! There's nothing left for you!"

"So you really did fuck him?" Alyssa asked with a look of disgust on her face. She walked up to me and got in my face. "How fucking dare you put your filthy, greasy little hands on my man. The whole school knows he's mine. How dare you corrupt him with your perverted ways!"

I smiled up at her, "He can't be yours if he's fucking me every night, now can he?" I had gotten brave at this point. Something about being punched in the face just makes you feel like nothing worse than that can happen at this point. So why the hell not?

Oliver laughs and pulls me into his side.

"I don't fucking believe it! There's no way you are actually dating him. This is just more bullshit to try and get rid of me."

At this point, I'm just done with Selena's bullshit. I wrap my arms around Oliver's neck and he gives me a startled expression as I crush my lips to his. I pull him closer to me, unable to get enough of him, and nibble as his bottom lip and run my tongue over it. Oliver opens his mouth for me and begins to devour me, thrusting his tongue inside.

Oliver was starting to get a little out of control as I felt his hands start to roam. This was just supposed to be a demonstration of my gayness, not an exhibition of our sex life. I pulled away from Oliver as I felt his hand snake up my shirt and his other grab my ass.

Everyone stood there in shock. Especially Alyssa and Selena.

Alyssa's face turned red as her gaze was drawn to Oliver's groin. I guess he was right; I do get him harder than a rock, I think to myself. I cough and Oliver turns to me, "Babe, you might wanna go do something about that." I say as I gesture to his now enlarged package.

He shrugs, "Only if you come help." A cocky grin starts to form on his face at his suggestive remark.

Selena screeches and storms off after our little show and Alyssa stands there dumbstruck.

She slowly turned to leave and I could have sworn I heard as she whispered, "He's huge." Under her breath. I laugh to myself and finally collapse into my chair at our table. Oliver does the same and we slowly pull our food towards us. Ignoring all the people's stares and whispers directed our way. At least we didn't have to hide it anymore.

24

OLIVER

I am being stared at. Everywhere. Does no one have anything better to do than gossip about my sex life? Every time I walk into a room it goes completely quiet and every time I leave a room whispers erupt behind me.

I went to grab my books for my homework out of my locker and it abruptly shut in my face, "So I hear you like dick, Miller."

I turn my head and see none other than the sly smile of Lucian Augur, "Lucian. It's been a while. Why are you even here? This isn't your school. Are you lost?"

Lucian rolls his eyes and says, "No I'm actually looking for someone right now. But don't worry I won't be here long." His eyes never stopped scanning the crowd.

"Well if you're looking for someone here then that can't be good. Nothing ever comes from associating with you."

His eyes light up as he finds what he's been searching so hard for, I turn around to see a flash of red hair in the distance as a girl took off and ran in the other direction. I don't know if Lucian could tell but it was very obvious that this girl did not want him to find her. 'That poor girl' is all I could think before Lucian was gone, chasing after her down the hallway.

I could see Raven as he grabbed his backpack and books out of his locker; I ran up behind him and wrapped my arms around his waist, with the secret out there was no reason to hide my feelings for him. I kissed his neck and whispered, "I need you at my place tonight. Preferably naked but I'll settle for you in my bed." The girl at the locker next to his looked at us with a grossed-out expression on her face and quickly closed her locker.

I felt Raven's laugh vibrate against my lips as I continued to kiss up and down his neck. "You know, even though we are out now that doesn't mean you can just grope me whenever you want. I feel like PDA is a bit unnecessary." He said as he placed another book in his bag.

"Yeah, but have you seen your ass in these jeans? I'm barely holding on as it is. You think I could restrain myself more?" I said discreetly brushing my groin against his ass.

Raven slowly turns in my arms and stands on his toes to whisper in my ear, "Then maybe it would help if I took them off? I wouldn't want you to suffer unnecessarily."

I moaned and captured his lips for a quick kiss.

"My house. Now." I said as I dragged him towards my car.

***

I push Raven against the wall as soon as we enter my dad's house. I kissed him hungrily, I haven't kissed him like this in a few days now. I needed it, I needed more. I pressed myself against him and pushed his jackets off his shoulders, my hands were moving on their own now as they glided up his shirt and tweaked a nipple. Raven rips his shirt off and then pulls mine over my head. I bring my lips back to his and slip my tongue in his mouth once more, loving the taste that was Raven.

I lifted Raven and he wrapped his legs around my waist. I secure my hands around his ass and carry him to my bedroom, leaving our clothes on the floor.

We burst through the door to my room and I kick the door shut as I toss Raven on my bed. I turn and lock the door; we wouldn't want any uninvited guests. I wanted Raven all to myself.

I turn around and slowly begin unbuttoning my jeans as I stare down as Raven's flushed face, swollen lips, and his disheveled hair after his beanie was knocked off when I tossed him. How can one person be so goddamn sexy? I pulled my pants down, exposing my erection, and watched as Raven bit his lip in anticipation.

I crawled onto the bed and slowly unbuttoned his pants and pulled them and his converse off. I've been thinking about stripping him naked all day, especially after that kiss in the cafeteria.

I pushed his legs back with my hands behind his knees and brought my mouth down to his hole. I flattened my tongue and gave slow, purposeful licks. I could hear Raven moan as I lapped my tongue on his sensitive asshole. I pointed my tongue and began fucking his ass with my tongue; loving the way his moans intensified with every thrust of my tongue. Raven brought his hand to his cock and began pumping it slowly; I smacked his hand away, only I was allowed to give him pleasure right now. I slowly started licking up his taint as I reached his balls and popped one, then the other, into my mouth, and gave a gentle suck. His cock twitched with pleasure and I slowly ran my tongue along his shaft until I reached the head. I gave it a gentle lick and then sucked it into my mouth. I sucked his delicious cock, swirling my tongue around his head every time I came up.

I continued sucking as I brought my finger to his ass and gently eased it in, earning an excited and earnest moan from Raven as I curled my finger and massaged his prostate. I began pumping in and out.

I felt Raven's breathing accelerate and his body tense, his orgasm imminent, and popped his dick out of my mouth.

"Oh no. You aren't allowed to cum yet." I said as I reached into my bedside drawer and brought out a cock ring. I slipped it onto his cock but instead of turning on the vibration, I tightened it, stopping Raven's ability to cum. "You can cum when I say so and not a second before."

Raven nodded silently. I brought my cock to his ass and after lubing it up I pushed into him. He moans loudly, his cock twitches, and I begin thrusting into his tight hole.

"Fuuuuck you're so tight," I say as I grip his thighs tightly. I start to lose control as I lean into him and begin slamming into his ass.

"Oliver, please!" Raven moans erotically as we move together.

"Please, what?"

"Please let me cum." Raven begs.

"I don't know. I don't think I'm ready to let you cum." I say as I grind my groin on his ass. Raven whines and spreads his legs wider. "And plus, I think you're enjoying this."

"Of course I am," he says breathlessly. "I love fucking you. I love your cock in my ass."

I slip out of his ass and lie on the bed, "Then show me how much you love it. Come ride me."

Raven crawls on top of me and crouches over my dick. He grips my base and slowly lowers himself onto my hard member. He gets halfway before I grip his hips and slam my cock into him.

"Fuck, Oliver." Raven moans as he begins fucking me.

I rest my hands behind my head leisurely and watch as Raven rides me. His cock bouncing every time he lowers himself onto me. Fuck, he feels so good.

"You look so sexy right now." I reach up and pinch his nipple. Raven moans loudly.

I feel my building orgasm as Raven rides me hard. I release Raven's cock and then sit up. I hold his ass in my hands and begin thrusting from underneath him quickly. Raven wraps his arms around my neck and brings his lips to mine. His kiss causes a chill to crawl up my spine and I lose it.

I flip him onto his stomach, his ass in the air, and thrust inside him once again.

"Fu-ck! You. Feel. So. Good!" Raven says with each thrust emphasizing his words.

"I fucking love you so much," I say as I fuck him hard and fast.

"Fuuuck Oliver I'm gonna cum!" he says as he grips the sheets.

"I'm right there with you, baby. Cum for me." I feel the sensation build and I fill his ass my hot load; Raven moans as he cums on my sheets. We collapse together and I plant a soft kiss on his lips.

"I love you."

"I love you too."

25

RAVEN

I went to grab my clothes to leave when Oliver pulled me back onto the bed, "Stay. I don't sleep well without you here with me."

I looked over my shoulder at him and said, "Fine but I get to be the little spoon this time, Miller." Oliver pumped his fists in the air in excitement. I crawl in bed next to him, and his arms wrap around my waist as I drift off to sleep.

***

I wake to two fingers in my ass; I pull the blankets back to find a grinning Oliver Miller between my legs. I moan as he finds my prostate and begins jerking my cock. I watch intently as he works his magic, never breaking eye contact. I bite my lip and he begins to jerk me off faster; I close my eyes in ecstasy. I feel something cold press against my asshole and I look down to find a small buttplug pressed against my entrance.

"We've got school in like twenty minutes," I laugh.

"Oh, I know. We'll be taking this with us." He says with an air of mischief. Realization washes over me. We are playing games today it seems.

"You aren't allowed to take this out today. Do you understand?" He asks as his eyes darkened with lust.

I swallow hard, "Yes, sir."

He sucks my cock into his mouth as he buries the butt plug in my ass; sucking quickly up and down bringing me to the edge quickly.

"Fuuuuuuuck," I moan as I cum hard in Oliver's mouth. He swallows and licks his lips.

I push him onto his back and slide down to his groin on my hands and knees, the butt plug gives me a full feeling as I pleasure Oliver.

I suck quickly; the time we need to leave for school ever-present in my mind. I place my hand at the base of his cock and jerk it up and down as I suck his huge cock.

Oliver's hands lace into my hair as my head bobs and grips tightly as he cums in my waiting mouth.

***

"Babe, can I borrow a shirt?" I call from the bathroom as I pull my jeans from yesterday back on. He throws me a 'Ramones' band t-shirt through the door and I catch it. I raise it to my nose and sniff; it smells like Oliver. I slip it over my head and pull my leather jacket on over it. I pull my beanie back on my head, sex hair is definitely not a look I want to sport my first day back after coming out in front of the whole school.

I step out of the bathroom and Oliver's eyes fixate on me, "You look good in my clothes."

"Thanks for letting me borrow it."

"That's one of my favorite shirts, okay? Take good care of it." He kisses me quickly and says, "Don't forget; you aren't allowed to take that plug out unless I say so. Alright, let's head out."

***

I walk into my class to Selena sitting on my desk.

110

"Selena . . . What can I do for you?" I ask as I plop down in my seat.

She looks me up and down and says, "I've never seen you in that shirt before. But you aren't fooling me, those jeans are the same you wore yesterday. I stared at your ass so I would know."

I meet her eyes and say, "The shirt's not mine. I didn't go home last night." I didn't want to beat around the bush with Selena. If I tried to spare her feelings she would never let me go.

She nodded in understanding, "It's his, isn't it." She said as she looked down.

"Yeah. It is."

"And I'm guessing if I took of that beanie I'd find sex hair, wouldn't I."

"More than likely. Seeing as how I fucked him last night and this morning." I said bluntly. This morning is brought to the front of my mind causing my asshole twitching around the plug.

Selena nodded and said, "Okay, Raven, I'm going to give up on you. But I would like it if we could be friends. I don't have any gay friends, and I like you. You aren't impressed by me. I have a feeling we would make great friends. And I have a feeling that you're the type who doesn't have many friends."

My eyes soften at the sincerity in her voice. "Okay. I'll be your friend." Her head snaps up in surprise at my words.

She throws herself at me in a hug and I tense up at her sudden outburst of affection. "Uuuuuh, can you not?" I ask uncomfortably.

"Oh! Sorry!" She says as she detaches herself from me. "I just didn't expect you to say yes. I guess you aren't a hugger?"

"Only with one person," I say as I rub my neck.

"Do you want to eat lunch together? I know you usually eat with Oliver but if you didn't mind if I joined you guys . . . "

"Actually, Oliver has weight lifting during lunch so I'm pretty free today."

Her face lit up in a bright smile at my words and she clapped excitedly, "Hell yeah. It's a date. Well . . . you know what I mean."

I laugh, "Yeah, I got you. Just meet me at the table from yesterday. That's where we usually sit."

I smiled to myself. It would be great if that was the end of that drama. The last thing I need is a stalker who wants into my pants.

***

After class, I stopped to go to the bathroom and as I walked past a stall I was abruptly pulled in. A hand covered my mouth as I was about to scream and a voice behind me whispered in my ear sending a shiver down my spine, "Drop your pants right now."

I shivered and slowly began to pull my pants down, not wanting any trouble. Fear was rushing through my veins as the unknown assailant slowly turned me towards him.

26

RAVEN

"Sorry, did I scare you?" Oliver whispered his smile fading as he met my eyes full of fear.

I smacked him on the arm, "Holy Hell, Oliver! You scared the fuck out of me!" His fingers started feather-like movements along my skin and my body started to relax.

He placed a gentle kiss on my lips and I melted. "I'm sorry. I didn't mean to scare you, baby."

My anger faded away at his sincerity and pecked another kiss to his lips, he smiled into my kiss and deepened it. I could feel his hands go down to my waist. He pushed me to the bathroom stall wall and pressed himself against me.

"How's my little present been treating you?" Oliver asked mischievously.

"Oh, it's been very stimulating, to say the least," I say and I suck his bottom lip into my mouth and bite lightly.

Oliver's eyes sparkle as he says, "Good because we aren't done yet." He reaches into his bag on the floor and pulls out another, bigger, butt plug. "I got you an upgrade."

I swallow and ask, "I'm supposed to keep that in for the rest of the day now?"

He kisses my neck, leaving a hickey, and says, "Uh-Huh. I better not catch u without it either."

He spins me around and bares my ass; the metal handle present between my cheeks. I feel his hands spread my ass and twist the butt plug earning a whimper from me. He slowly pulls it out, leaving me with an empty feeling. I feel a cold liquid on my ass as he pours more lube on my gaping hole and slowly inserts the larger butt plug into my waiting hole and it swallows it eagerly. I moan at the full feeling, my dick coming to life at the stimulation. Oliver cleans up the excess lube and turns me towards him.

"Don't you dare touch yourself. Do you understand me?"

"Yes, sir," I respond obediently, loving how dominating Oliver can be.

"Pull your pants up then," Oliver says as he leaves the stall abruptly, shutting it behind him, leaving me red-faced and hard as a rock.

I pull my pants on and leave the restroom, still blushing, as I go to meet Selena for lunch.

***

"What's going on with your face?" Selena asks as I sit down next to her.

"What do you mean?" I ask as I pretend to not know what she's talking about, surely she can't know what happened already.

Her eyes narrowed and she said, "Well you are red as a beet; you look embarrassed or guilty, one or the other . . . . . Then there's also the hickey."

I bury my face in my hands and say, "I ran into Oliver a couple of minutes ago so. . . .I'm sure you can guess what happened."

Selena smiles and says, "Nooooo don't tell me you guys did it in the bathroom! You are so bad! Details! Tell me; I want to know everything!"

I blushed thinking about our rendezvous. "We didn't have sex or anything. He kind of just pulled me into a bathroom stall to make out." And other things but she doesn't need to know about the butt plug that's in my ass, every clench my ass makes around it is sending pleasure to my already straining member. I hope to god no one notices my raging hard-on.

"Is he a good kisser?" Selena asks as she leans towards me, eager for my answer.

I lay my head on the table, "So fucking good. It should be a crime." I answer honestly.

"How's the sex?" She asked curiously.

"Amazing. For me being his first guy; he's incredible. His stamina is amazing, probably from swimming," She nods in agreement, "And his libido is so high we are almost always fucking."

"Is he . . . You know . . . big?" She blushes at her question.

"Huge. Definitely above average." I lean forward and whisper, "And between just you and me, Oliver is extremely possessive and kinky."

Her eyes widened, "Really? I would have just thought Oliver was a clumsy vanilla type."

"Absolutely not." I shake my head.

"Maybe all the girls in school can just sense his big dick energy," she laughs. "And that's why everyone is so interested in him."

"I mean even if that wasn't true; Just look at him, he has a gorgeous face, a sexy body, and he's tall. Everyone would obviously want o fuck that. I mean his eyes alone could get me in bed. And they kind of did."

Selena shrugs, "I've always been more of a brown eyes type of girl." I glanced at her discreetly, hopefully she wasn't talking about me.

I drop her off at her classroom and wave as I head to mine. "I'll see you tomorrow," I say as she opens her classroom door. She smiles, nods, and closes the door behind her.

27

OLIVER

"Raven, hurry up, we're gonna be late!" I yell from the living room as I check myself out in the mirror, not a hair out of place.

Raven walks out of his room and says, "You can't be late to a party, Oliver. You just show up whenever." My jaw dropped, my mouth watering, as I stared at the adonis before me. My eyes land first on his beanie covered head; his hair is getting kind of long, he should probably get it cut. Then they trail down to his black and white, unbuttoned, plaid, flannel over a paint-splattered v-neck with a silver chain around his neck. He wore a pair of dark wash skinny jeans with the knees ripped out, tucked into black leather combat boots. His ring was safely on his finger.

"That's it we aren't going," I announce as I pull Raven into my arms.

"Oliver, I did NOT get dressed up just for you to tell me we aren't going. It took me thirty minutes to muster enough energy to be able to go through this level of social interaction. Selena invited me, I said I would go. End of story. Now get that sexy ass in the car." He yelled as he slapped my ass with enough force to jolt me. I chuckled inwardly. God, I love him.

RAVEN

We walked into the party and it seemed like everyone's eyes were on us. I saw a redhead of hair amid the crowd and I dragged Oliver forward. "Selena!" I yelled trying to get her attention over the loud music.

Her eyes landed on me and she screamed, "Raven! You made it!" She rushed over and launched herself on me wrapping me in her arms. Her strong perfume filled my lungs, but it wasn't bad. She smelled like cinnamon and vanilla.

Oliver coughed at the prolonged hug and she finally released me. "OMG and you brought Oliver! That's perfect! We are about to start a drinking game so this makes an even amount of people playing!"

"What game are we playing?" I ask. I know you might not be able to tell based on how comfortable I seem in social situations but I have never played a drinking game.

"Thunderstruck! So the way it works is we play the song 'Thunderstruck' and everyone takes turns drinking when it says thunderstruck in the song and you have to keep drinking until it says it again and then it's the next person's turn to drink!"

'Great.' I think to myself.

We gather around the table in the living room with cups of beer spread out in front of each person. Oliver and I take a seat and a short, curly-haired kid with freckles scattered across his nose takes the seat next to me. He had a smudge of grease on his cheek and an impish like grin that gave me the impression he was up to no good.

"Hey, how's it going? My name's Leo!" He said as he shook my hand. His eyes connected with Oliver and he smiled brightly.

"Oliver! What's up? I haven't seen you since that day when you came to get all that stuff for your girlfriend!" My face reddens at that when I think of how technically I am Oliver's 'girlfriend' and the things Oliver has bought for me haven't exactly been PG.

"Um, where exactly do you work?" I ask.

"Well, that depends. By day I work at the auto body shop *'The Forge'* as a mechanic but by niiiight I work at *Toys of Sexual Torture.* That is a XXX store where I work as a cashier. Oliver was there before Christmas break buying some very suspicious things." He said as he wiggles his eyebrows in a suggestive manner.

Oliver throws his arm over my shoulder and leans towards Leo and says, "Hey man, don't be telling everyone all my secrets, my boyfriend won't like it if everyone knows what goes on behind closed doors." Leo's eyes move to me and nod in understanding.

"Now I know why you were so cryptic when I asked about your girlfriend," he laughed.

"Yeah, we haven't been public for very long," Oliver explained.

Selena plops down on the couch and announces, "Alright guys; we will be moving clockwise starting with me, everyone has been told the rules. Let's get started!" She starts the music and picks up her cup.

***

I was falling all over Leo by the end of the game; I got screwed over when it hit the guitar solo on my turn, and now I was having issues standing.

"I gotta go take a leak," I say slurring my words. I stumble my way toward the bathroom and shut the door. As soon as I start to relieve myself the bathroom door opens and arms wrap around my waist.

"Come on, Oliver. I'm trying to pee. Leave me alone." I say with half-lidded eyes. Everything was blurry and I was seeing double. I barely get myself taken care of before I'm turned around abruptly, making my world spin from the momentum. I didn't have enough time to process my surroundings before someone's lips were on mine. They were so soft and tasted like strawberries. Wait . . . Strawberries? I opened my eyes to see a tall brunette, the same one I saw when I was hiding from Alyssa in the hallway.

I pulled away and asked, "Who the fuck are you? You aren't Oliver." She was on me again immediately and, because things couldn't get any worse, Oliver opens the bathroom door.

"Raven are you -" He stopped mid-sentence at the scene that was unfolding before him. He looks between the two of us, eyes focusing on my still undone pants and my exposed groin, and slams the door shut. I hurriedly buttoned up my pants and ran out the door to try and find Oliver, but he was gone.

"Hey Raven, did you and Oliver get in a fight? I just saw him leaving pissed as fuck."

I punch the wall next to me and say, "Yeah I saw him. Or rather he saw me, right as some brunette stuck her tongue down my throat while I was going to the bathroom. I don't even know who that bitch is!" I sigh, "Hey do you think you could drive me home? Oliver was my ride."

Leo looks towards the bathroom right as the brunette walks out with a satisfied look on her face and says, "Was that the girl?"

"Yeah, I've never seen her in my life. Maybe she's wasted."

"That's Hylie. Alyssa Davis' sister. She's in my health class."

Realization crashes over me like a wave and I throw my beanie on the ground in anger. "Of fucking course it is! Why wouldn't Alyssa be the cause of this? I was fucking set up! And now Oliver thinks I'm cheating on him!"

"Well, why don't I drive you home and then you can talk to Oliver in the morning when he has a chance to calm down. Because I doubt we will be willing to talk to you now."

"You're probably right." I sigh.

"Let's go! Festus awaits!"

"You named your car Festus?"

"Hell yeah, I did. I built it myself, starting with just a chassis. I did the wiring and even the paint job." Leo said proudly as we approached a truck with a dragon painted on the side.

28

RAVEN

The next morning came and I felt like death. Literal death. I pulled on a random pair of jeans and an oversized slipknot t-shirt and headed to school. I wasn't trying to look good today, I wasn't in the mood. I look at Leo sleeping on the couch and write him a note:

I'm headed off to school.

Lock the door before you leave.

Text me when you head out.

347-262-9275

-Raven

Every clank of the locker's closing doors caused a wave of pain to crash down on my vulnerable brain. I winced as someone closed mine as I pulled my books out. I rubbed my temples and looked at Selena.

"Oh. It's you. What's up?" I grumble through my throbbing headache.

"Wow. What a warm welcome from my friend after I invite you to my amazing party." Selena says sarcastically.

"Yeah well, I'm hungover as fuck. Who throws a party on a Thursday anyway?"

"This beautiful bitch right here. Don't act like you didn't enjoy yourself. I heard from a little birdie you were caught making a phone call to the goddess of love herself in the bathroom. I guess you aren't as gay as you thought you were." Selena says with a giggle and a shrug.

"No that's not what happened. It was more like I got jumped while taking a leak and now Oliver thinks I'm fucking someone on the side. I haven't even seen him yet to explain what happened. Although, this wouldn't be the first time something like this has happened so, hopefully, he believes me." I groan as I drag my hands down my face. I should have just stayed home.

My phone beeps and I see and text from an unknown number light up my screen.

Unknown: *Thanks for letting me crash last night.*

Raven: *Leo?*

Leo: *Well of course. Unless you handed your number to another devilishly handsome Latino when you were wasted last night.*

Raven: *I don't think I gave my number to ANYONE devilishly handsome. I would have remembered that.*

Leo: *Oof. Ouch. That hurts. Damn, Raven, I thought we were friends.*

Raven: *I'm about to head to class. Do you not have school?*

The dots danced for what felt like forever when he finally responded.

Leo: *I dropped out last year when my mom died. I've just been working now.*

That explains how he has enough time to be a mechanic by day and a sex toy cashier by night. I stare at the text for a while

Raven: *We should hang out more. Feel free to stop by my place any time.*

Leo sends me a thumbs up as my teacher begins class and I tuck my phone away.

***

I walk into my third period to find Selena sitting on my desk swinging her legs. "So have you talked to Oliver today?" she asks as I lower myself into my seat.

"No. I haven't seen him at all. He hasn't stopped at my locked once, hasn't been waiting outside any of my classes like usual, and he isn't responding to my text messages." I lay my head in her lap and she starts playing with my messy hair. "I don't really know what to do anymore. I doubt if I went to his house he'd even open the door. I'm just hoping at this point that he's sitting at our lunch table after this."

I feel a chill crawl up my spine and I look up at the door; Oliver was standing there, and he didn't look happy. He didn't look mad either, more like - heartbroken.

I stand abruptly and rush out of my classroom and he turns to leave.

"Oliver, wait!" I yell as he starts to run. He stops and turns slowly with his head down low.

"I've been looking for you everywhere." I take a step toward him and he takes a step back.

"I have a schedule, Raven. Obviously you weren't looking hard enough." He raised his head and I could see a sea of hurt within them.

"That wasn't what it looked like," I explained.

"What? The part where I caught you with your dick out and tongue down a girl's throat or you snuggled up to Selena, your so-called-friend?" His brows furrowed and he turned to leave again.

I grab his arm to stop him and say, "None of it. It was a set-up. Leo told me that the girl was Hylie, Alyssa's sister. She was the one who took our picture in the cafeteria. You have to believe me, Oliver. I'd never cheat on you. Especially not with a girl. Did you ever stop to realize that my dick wasn't even hard? She jumped me while I was taking a piss."

"And with Selena? Was that a set-up too? Because you guys looked really cozy. Almost like a couple. I don't understand, Raven. Was what we had just a game for you? Just trying to make the straight guy fall in love with you and then throw him away after he admits his feelings in front of the whole school?" Oliver was mad now. My heart ached as he exposed all his uncertainties.

"Oliver this isn't a game to me! It never was! I love you, you just have to trust me!"

"Raven I do trust you but when I see you with my own eyes it gets hard. If it was just a rumor you know I'd be on your side but it's right here in front of me; I can't just ignore it."

"Ask Leo! He was there; he saw too. He knows. He even drove me home. Selena will tell you too. She didn't believe me at first but she does now. What you saw before was just her comforting me while I was talking about how I couldn't find you. I was going to use my free period to go look for you. I can't just skip my classes. I don't have good enough grades for that."

Oliver looked down at his feet and sighed, "I just - I need some time. You have no idea how much that hurt me. I've always put a solid line between me and everyone else, I've made it plainly clear to everyone that I was taken. You know that."

Tears sprung into my eyes at his words and I choked out, "Are you breaking up with me?"

Oliver's eyes widened. "Of course not! I just need some space. Just wait for me to come to you."

I breathed out a sigh of relief. "Okay. I can do that. I can give you space. Just promise me one thing. I'm still yours, right? And you're still mine?"

Oliver pulls me into a hug and says, "I don't think there's ever going to be something you could do that would change that. Just - draw that line okay? I get jealous, you know that."

He pulls away and I feel completely alone from the absence of his warmth. He turns to walk away and I crumple to the floor.

29

OLIVER

"So you broke up with him?" Jaxon asked after I finished telling him everything that had happened.

"Not exactly. I told him I needed space." I say before I shove a handful of ships into my mouth.

"I guess that explains why you called me to hang out. You guys have been connected at the hip ever since you first started dating. Do you guys even do actual dates? I only ever hear of you staying in and having sex." He says as he leans back on the couch.

"We have real dates. We went to the movies a while ago and a party the other day. That's how this shit started."

"Wait what party? I didn't get the party-goer vibe from Raven when we talked so I wouldn't think he'd even want to go to one."

"His friend Selena invited him. I didn't want to go. I just wanted to stay home and have sex. You know, the usual, but he was like 'No I promised I'd go so you are too.'"

"Selena . . . . Baker?"

"Yeah . . . Wait how do you know her?"

"She's got a . . . reputation. I remember her from a few parties Alyssa threw back when Alyssa was going to my school. They just hung out every so often so I'm sure she's fine, but then there's the issue of when she gets a crush. I mean rumors aren't always true, but every time she gets attracted to a guy she calls it the 'call of the goddess of love'. She thinks it's fate and that's the end of the story. She does whatever is necessary to get the guy. From what you told me before; it sounds like she's got a liking for Raven, so I'd lookout. Raven is hard-stuck gay; so he's not the one you have to worry about, but it would suck if something were to happen to him. In my opinion, if Raven says that nothing happened and that it was a setup, I'd believe him. You were the one that got him in this love square in the first place. No one even knew Raven existed until you decided to grope him in public and now all of a sudden everything is blowing up in your face."

I sigh in exasperation, "You're right." I put my head in my hands. "This is all my fault."

"How did Raven get home from that party anyway if you abandoned him?" Jaxon asked as he took a drink of his soda.

"My friend Leo took him home. Apparently he also saw Hylie leaving the scene of where Raven says she jumped him in the bathroom."

"Hylie, like Alyssa's sister Hylie?"

"Yeah. She was the one with her tongue down his throat."

"Okay, yeah, this is definitely a setup. Hylie HATES guys. In her mind, men are only good for what she needs to get the job done. Nothing more. I definitely don't think that Hylie would choose Raven as a sexy one-night stand type of guy. And another connection to Alyssa? Suspicious as fuck. I'm surprised it took you this long to connect all the dots. I think all that chlorine from the pool is fucking with your brain."

"Fuck! I'm a fucking idiot!"

"I know, now what are you still doing here? Go get your man."

I scramble out of my chair and grab my coat and keys. I run out the door and hop in my front seat; the passenger door opens and Jaxon sits down next to me.

"You're coming too?"

"Well, someone's gotta make sure you don't fuck it up this time, right?"

I laugh and start the car. "Good, because we both know I totally could. That's to say if I haven't already."

***

JAXON

"Wait, don't you think we should knock first?" I say as Oliver goes to turn the door handle.

"No, if I knock he might not answer," he says as he reaches again.

"And if he's not even home and you trigger the security system?" I reason.

Oliver stops. "Okay, then what do you suggest?"

I pull out my phone and begin to dial, "Call Cassie." I shrug.

The phone rings for a moment before not Cassie, but Frank, answers the phone. "Frank, hey, is Cassie there?"

Yeah, she's in the shower. Do you need me to get her?

"Can you just ask her if Raven's home?"

Gimme a second. . . . . She said he should be. He had a friend over last night.

"Okay, thanks," I say as I hang up.

"So he's home. But he isn't alone." I say as I appraised Oliver's reaction. His fist clenches and I say, "Remember what we just talked about. Raven isn't that type of person. So don't jump to conclusions."

He lets out a deep breath to calm himself and reaches for the handle once again. This time I didn't stop him.

***

RAVEN

I step out of the shower and wrap a towel around my waist as I hear the front door open. 'Cassie must be home.' I think to myself and go to say hi. But it wasn't Cassie. It was Oliver; and he was standing in the living room glaring daggers at Leo's back. He was laying curled up, facing the back of the couch, still sleeping.

Oliver's eyes landed on my towel-clad body and I knew what was going through his mind. This had all happened before, after all. As Oliver rushed angrily towards me, Jaxon who was standing behind Oliver rushed to the sleeping Leo. He threw him over his shoulder and ran out the door. I'm not surprised. He was a victim of Oliver's jealous rage. He obviously believed I wasn't at fault for everything happening and decided that he'd save Leo the pain.

"Who was he?!" Oliver yelled.

30

RAVEN

"Sit down." Oliver virtually snarled. His anger ignited a surprising urge to be obedient within me. I sat down immediately. As I sat my towel came undone from around my waist and flopped to the floor. My still hard dick slapped against my stomach.

Although his face still depicted pure rage, for reasons I still wasn't clear on, his eyes had a strange glint in them, almost as if he was enjoying himself. His eyes trailed down my body and once they reached my quivering thighs he instructed me to get on my hands and knees. Loving the way he was dominating me, I complied without daring to ask any questions. He stood and began trailing his hands over my body, gently at first, then he began slapping my ass repeatedly. My heart hammered away inside my chest, and my breath quickened and became shallow. I felt as if I would come before Oliver even entered me.

"You're going to have to relax if I'm going to put anything inside of you," Oliver said as he stuck a finger into my tight asshole.

"Ah! Oliver . . . you're gonna use lube, right?"

"I don't know. I'm still angry with you."

He pulled his belt off and dragged me into my room. He threw me onto the bed and then climbed on right behind me. He sat me up against the headboard and then pulled my legs up by my shoulders. He wrapped the belt around my wrists and then through the open spaces in the molding. It was clear that I was not going to be moving from this spot for a while.

Once Oliver was done, he sat back and glowered at me.

The position I was in wasn't exactly uncomfortable, although it would've been more comfortable if it hadn't been a leather belt retraining me.

I looked at Oliver and said, "Only you can do these things to me."

Oliver left the room and returned with his backpack from his car. He reached inside and pulled out a monster dildo and thankfully some lube.

"I had brought these things for some kinky make-up sex but that didn't go as planned. I want you to feel pain right now, but I love your ass too much to destroy it. So, lucky for you, I'm going to use lube." He said while slathering up the dildo and then my ass. He squirted more onto his fingers and then worked them inside of my ass, getting the lube past my tight ring, which had begun to grow accustomed to the frequent intrusions, each thrust from his fingers causing my dick to rise and harden. Then I felt something plastic, and foreign, press against my hole.

"Ah! Oliver . . . please, be gentle." I begged desperately. I knew Oliver wouldn't intentionally hurt me, but this person in front of me wasn't Oliver. Oliver - with his carefree attitude, sarcastic smile, and gentle touch - had been stolen away by this animal, driven by rage and lust, in front of me. And the thing that scared me the most was that I didn't mind. The idea of pain brought me pleasure just thinking about it, as long as Oliver was the one inflicting it I didn't care.

Then Oliver began to work the dildo into my ass, slowly at first but then he started to slam it in. To be honest, I almost came just from him putting it in.

"Ah! God i - damn, Oliver! It - It's too big!" I panted.

"Yeah, Raven. But you like it don't you, you fucking whore. Come on. Tell me, it feels good doesn't it?"

"Ah! Ah! Nng! God, yes! Yes, Oliver! It feels good!" I screamed as I came to the brink of coming.

"How many people are you showing this lewd expression to? Did you show it to that bastard that was here earlier?"

"Ah - what? No, no one else! Only you. There has only ever been you! I don't love anyone other than you." And as those lost words escaped my mouth, I came. I looked down to see my cum splattered across my stomach.

Oliver just sat there for a moment. He watched me as I breathed heavily before he spoke again.

"Do you really love me?" He asked doubtfully.

"Yes, Oliver. I love you. I've been in love with you this entire time. I've been in love with you since the first time I saw you swim. It's the reason why I can never stay mad at you for too long. It's the reason why I do these kinds of things with you. It's the reason why I could never cheat on you, it would be too painful."

I watched Oliver's face soften before he looked at me and smiled his cocky grin that I loved so much and said, "I love you too."

My face lit up at the sound of his loving words. It made me happy to see his smile return to his face. Even though I might be a masochist, the sadist look really doesn't fit Oliver. Although I do think he might've had fun in the process. Then I began to realize my discomfort.

"Um, Oliver? Can you untie me now?"

The glimmer returned to his eyes again as he looked at me, his eyes drifted down to my exposed area, and he said, "But I wasn't done yet. I'd hate for all of these toys to go to waste." He then began pulling out all of the other sex toys. With each one he placed on the bed my dick raised another inch. By the time he finished, I was fully erect.

"It doesn't look like you want to be untied."

"Only you can make me like this."

"Oh really? Then I guess I should fix it, shouldn't I?" He said as he grasped my dick and inhaled it into his mouth.

"Ah - Nng. Oliver - feels . . . Ah!" The suction that Oliver was applying began to drive me insane. The feeling of his hot mouth sucking my cock was amazing. Each stroke of my penis sent a shiver down my spine pushing me closer and closer to my orgasm.

"What? Feels good? What about when I touch you here . . . ?" He asked as he fondled my balls and then inserted a finger into my twitching hole.

The pleasure stole away my voice. I was already sensitive from my orgasm, so I came once his finger slipped past my tight ring.

I lied there gasping and hoping for a short break. But then Oliver slipped the vibrating ring over my limp dick.

"Wha - What are you doing?" I asked nervously.

He looked at me with a shining smirk on his face and said, "Don't worry. I'm only gonna make you feel good from now on. After all, we love each other don't we?" I wasn't able to answer because as he said the last word he turned on the vibrating ring and a shock pulsed through me. Then he reached to grab the anal pill and slowly slipped it inside of me and turned it on. My back arched in pleasure. I strained against the chains. The pleasure made my vision start to blur as the vibrations coursed through me. My eyes connected with Oliver's and I watched as he stroked his cock while watching me fight against my rising orgasm. My dick started to twitch and then I came so hard I saw spots. Oliver then leaned forward and kissed me hard on the lips. His tongue slipped into my mouth and he explored my mouth. I didn't have the energy to fight against his tongue for dominance. I just allowed him to swirl around in my mouth and delighted at the feeling of it. His tongue caressed mine, then he pulled away, and pecked me on the lips.

He pulled out the vibrating anal pill and removed the ring after turning it off. He tossed everything to the side, cleaned my stomach, and then began unchaining me. Once the belt were removed I slumped to the side. I felt the bed jostle as Oliver moved to lie behind me and put his arms around me. As he came closer I felt his hard-on against my thigh.

"Wait, what about you?" I asked softly.

"Don't worry about it, I'll be fine."

I didn't think it was fair that he made me come so many times but he never even came once, so I turned around to face Oliver, and then I wiggled my way down to his midsection. I took his member in my hands. I heard him gasp at my touch, understandable seeing as how he was almost ready to burst. I lightly licked the tip of his cock and then slowly pulled it into my mouth. Slowly at first, and then faster, I worked my hands in unison with my mouth over his dick. Working to make him come as he had with me. I reached one of my hands in between his thighs and fondled his balls. His balls became tight and I knew he was close to coming.

"Raven, let go. I'm gonna come."

"That's fine. Come."

I worked my mouth over his cock faster, bobbing my head. Then Oliver exploded and his cum flooded my mouth. I swallowed it and then licked the remainder off of my lips.

Oliver then pulled me up to face him and kissed me lightly on the lips and said, "I love you."

I looked back at him and said, "I love you too."

Jaxon and Leo, of course, chose this moment to walk in my room. "Hey, Raven did you guys make-up - Fuck, my bad." They go to leave but Oliver already has his pants on and is rushing towards Leo, who he hasn't recognized yet.

31

RAVEN

"Oliver, sit down," I said, my eyes and heart hardening. I was tired of him not trusting me. Every time something happens he completely flips his switch. "First of all, this is my house. I can invite anyone I want to my house. I don't have to ask for your permission. It doesn't matter what gender they are or whether or not you think I might sleep with them. If you don't trust me, that's your problem." My words caused him to still as Jaxon and Leo flinch from his aggressive advances.

"I told you that you needed to draw the line between friends and me; to make it obvious that they didn't have a chance with you, but you can't seem to do that," Oliver said as his anger rose.

"You still aren't getting it! Just because someone is in my house doesn't mean that I'm willing to sleep with them!"

"Then who was that?!" Oliver yells.

"And this is why I came with you, Oliver. You're fucking it up again. Raven didn't do anything wrong." Jaxon says while giving Oliver a look of disappointment.

Oliver's eyes fall on Leo, finally recognizing him through his angry haze that has been clouding his judgment, and he puts his face in his hands, "I'm a fucking idiot, aren't I?"

"Yeah," We all say in unison.

Oliver pulls me into a hug and apologizes but my arms don't move from my side. The only reason he was apologizing was because SOMEONE ELSE showed I was innocent; not because he trusted me on his own. He feels my body become unresponsive and looks down at me. "Raven?" He asks as his brows furrowed in confusion.

"What? Just because Jaxon says something now everything is all better? Why is it that it took someone else to say you are being ridiculous for you to calm down, but when I'm saying how that isn't what happened you won't believe me?" I push Oliver away and go to my room slamming the door behind me.

I start throwing clothes on and then I hear a knock at my door. I pull it open to tell Oliver to fuck off, but it wasn't him. On the other side of the door stood Jaxon.

"Hey, can we talk?" Jaxon asks. I gesture for him to come in, shooting a glare at Oliver as he sits down on the couch.

Jaxon sits down on the bed and sighs heavily. "He's such a fucking idiot. We were coming here for him to tell you that he was wrong and that he trusts you. But of course, he had to go and fuck it up." He looks up at me and blushes. "Raven, can you . . . . put on more clothes."

I looked down and realized I had only pulled on boxers and a wife-beater before answering the door. "Why does it matter, Jaxon? It's not like you care about my appearance. You're straight."

"Um, well - about that. I might not be," he says as he diverts his gaze.

I pull a t-shirt and jeans on quickly and say, "What do you mean 'you might not be'?"

"Well, I've been having some . . . . . reactions. I already broke up with Piper because of them." He says turning redder. "I actually really like your friend out there. What's his name?"

"Leo Rodriquez. So he's your type? I don't know if he's gay or not so you might have to do some whooing." I say while wiggling my eyebrows.

"Wait . . . . Leo . . . . Rodriquez? He doesn't happen to work at 'The Forge' does he?"

I look at him with raised eyebrows and say, "Yeeeeaaaah, why?"

"Nothing. Don't worry about it." He says. His reaction is so weird. "Anyway, is there any way that you can give him another chance. He's just stupid and lets his emotions get the better of him."

"I don't know. He doesn't trust me, he is overly-possessive and goes crazy when I talk to people. I'm starting to think our relationship is toxic." I say as I lean against my bedroom wall.

"No, trust me, you guys are perfect together. My relationship with Piper was rotting from the inside so I can tell from experience that it isn't the same. Oliver just needs to get his head out of his ass and start treating you the way you deserve to be treated. He loves you; and I know you love him."

"Do you think he's even capable of that kind of change?"

"He's going to have to be if he wants to keep you," Jaxon says as he gets up to leave. "I'm not saying you should react as if nothing happened. I'm just saying give that fish-for-brains another chance and I'll make sure he doesn't fuck it up again." The door shuts behind him and I'm left completely alone with my thoughts.

32

OLIVER

"What are you doing here, Leo?" I ask as Jaxon enters Raven's room.

"I felt like I should come back and help Raven explain. After I woke up Jaxon told me how I should just run for it but I knew that would just cause more trouble for Raven in the long run so I convinced Jaxon to come back with me." Leo shrugged. "I promise we weren't doing anything, man. Raven has just been helping me out. I kind of . . . . ran away from my foster home. That's why I haven't been to school and why I've been working so much. Raven has been letting me crash on the couch since his parents are out of town so much." He gestures to his duffle bag next to the couch.

I sigh heavily. I've really fucked up. Only I could take Raven's good dead and turn it into a cheating scandal. "It's good that Jaxon took you away. I get crazy jealous and I probably would have hurt you if he hadn't. I'm happy you came back though. You're a good friend. Raven needs more of those." I punch him lightly on the shoulder and smile.

Jaxon walks out of Raven's room and gives me a pained smile. "Dude, you have a lot of making up to do. He's thinking of dumping you." My eyes widen. Dumping me? I mean I understand that I fucked up but was it that bad?

Jaxon meets my eyes and practically reads my thoughts when he says, "Yeah it's that fucking bad, Oliver! This isn't the first time you've jumped to conclusions. There was the time with Hylie, Selena, and now Leo. You can't try to kill everyone that comes into contact with Raven. Relationships don't work that way. You are being too overbearing. I've asked him to give you another chance but there are no guarantees. He said he would think about it. Just how he didn't say yes immediately is proof enough that you're on the ropes. I don't think I can help you out of this mess." Jaxon shakes his head and goes to leave. "Come on. You need to give him space. I doubt he wants to see you when he opens that door."

"What if I talk to him?" Leo asks.

"You would do that? Even after I had full intentions of beating the shit out of you?" I asked in disbelief.

"Yeah. I mean I kind of caused this unintentionally, and you guys are my friends. I would hate for this to be what breaks you guys up."

"You didn't cause this, Leo. I did. Me and my fucking stupidity. If you want to help I'd be grateful but don't do it because you feel guilty." I put my hands on his shoulders and say, "It isn't your job to fix my mistakes."

"Hey, we're friends aren't we? I just want Raven to be happy. And I know being with you makes him happy. He just needs some help remembering that right now." Leo says as he walks towards Raven's bedroom door.

***

LEO

"Let me guess. You want me to forgive Oliver too?" Raven asked as he shut his bedroom door.

"Naw I just wanted to know about the blonde in your living room," I ask as I wiggle my eyebrows suggestively.

Raven bursts out laughing and asks, "So you're gay?"

"No," I laugh. "I just wanted to diffuse the tension. I'm more of a personality kind of guy. Gender doesn't matter. But from what I can tell he's a good guy underneath all the bravado. But you and I both know I'm not in the position to be dating. I need to get myself in a better situation first."

Raven nods understandingly. "He asked about you too." He smiles as he nods towards the door.

I gasp sarcastically, "Raven Weber! Sharing a friend's secrets? How dare you!" I put my hand over my mouth in mock horror but smiled widely.

"So why are you here?" Raven asks and the conversation turns serious.

"My friends are hurting. I want to fix it. But I gotta say troubleshooting machines is a lot easier than humans." I say as I rub my neck awkwardly. "When machines break there's always a way to fix it. So now I'm just hoping this isn't too broken for me to fix."

Raven's eyes soften and he sighs, "This isn't something you need to fix, Leo."

"Doesn't mean I'm not going to try. You're helping me, now I help you." I pull Raven into a hug and say, "Even through all the bullshit he makes you happy, don't let this get between you guys. You both know that it's Alyssa causing all these problems so now do something about it. Either let her keep driving a wedge between you or finally shut her up. I'm not there to protect you. So you guys need to band together and trust no one other than each other. No matter what you guys see, if the other says something isn't right believe them. One hundred percent trust." I pull away and smile. "If you guys stand together there isn't anything that can separate you."

I playfully punch Raven in the shoulder and say, "Now I've got to go to work but I'll see you later."

RAVEN

I stood outside Oliver's house and took a deep breath. 'I can do this.' I thought to myself as I grabbed the handle turned.

141

I walked in to find Oliver pushing Alyssa away as she lunged to kiss him.

"Get away from me!" Oliver yelled as he threw pillows at her from a distance.

"You were fine kissing me when you were asleep, why can't you just kiss me now?" She yelled back as she gave another desperate lunge.

"I thought you were Raven. I can't control my reactions when I'm asleep, Alyssa! How did you even get inside my house?!" Oliver dodged once again and I just stood there silently taking in the scene.

"I copied your keys while you were at swim practice, duh." How did she not realize what was wrong with that statement? Was she fucking insane?

Alyssa finally makes a lucky lunge and tackles Oliver to the ground. She braces her knees on his arms above his elbows and he's pinned down. She pulls off her shirt and moves to kiss him, Oliver was flailing underneath her in a useless effort to get free. I could no longer sit idly when I saw her reach behind herself to grope at his crotch. I grab her hair and pull her off of him, leaving Oliver completely stunned.

She screamed as I dropped her to the front door and threw her shirt at her. "Get the fuck out you desperate whore." I growl, barely able to contain my anger.

She cowers and quickly starts pulling her shirt back on. She begins to cry and sobs, "Why am I not attractive enough for you?"

Oliver's eyes soften and he stands up. He walks over to her and says, "Because I belong to someone else. I always have." Oliver reaches for me and touches my hand. I smile at him and take his hand in mine.

"Alyssa you've got to stop this. Everything you are doing isn't going to win Oliver over. In fact, you're driving him away faster. If you had just calmed down maybe you guys could have been friends, but not when it is so obvious you have feelings for him. Being friends or even just being around him will just hurt you in the long run. The happier Oliver and I get the more miserable you'll become. The best thing for you is to move on; because I'm not giving him up to anyone."

Alyssa got up and gave a silent nod before she reached for the handle. She paused for a moment and turned back to Oliver, "I'm sorry. Everything was my fault. I won't bother you anymore." She closes the door behind her.

Oliver gives a sigh of relief and then looks at me, "I promise I thought it was you while I was sleeping, but something didn't feel right and when I woke up -"

I stopped his rambling with a kiss as I threw myself against him. "I don't care. I trust you. I know you wouldn't do something like that on purpose. It's fine." Oliver relaxed into my arms and gave a sigh of relief.

"Where did she touch you? I have to erase everything." I said as my hands began to roam. A spark came into Oliver's eyes as he scooped me into his arms and started to run towards his room.

"What are you doing?"

"Well if you are going to erase everything I'd rather you do it somewhere I can do something about it. Seeing as how my dad will be home any minute." He says as he nibbles my ear.

He lowered me onto the bed and slowly covered my body with his. My hands begin to roam as he locks his lips to mine. My body lights on fire everywhere he touches and my cock begins to harden.

"Mmmm I feel something," Oliver mumbles against my lips. "I feel like I've been starving for your touch."

I tear at Oliver's shirt as I feel the desperate need to touch him. He begins peeling my clothes away, our lips never breaking contact. As I lay naked beneath him, Oliver breaks our kiss and stares down at my bare body, "You are stunning." He whispers.

He brings his lips to my neck and I feel his fingers leaving a light trail to my hole. He begins rubbing me before he eventually slips a finger inside. I moan at the feeling and he adds another finger.

"Your hole is practically swallowing me." He mumbles against my neck.

"That's because you feel so good," I moan.

I spread my legs wider, giving him more access as his fingers deliver delicious torture to my quivering hole. I need more.

"Oliver, please." I gasp.

"Mmmmm what's that, baby?" Oliver asks as he angles his fingers and begins rubbing my prostate with every thrust of his fingers.

"More please," I beg. Oliver adds another finger and I feel my hole stretch. "Faster," I beg and Oliver's fingers begin thrusting into me faster. It's not enough.

"Oliver please!" I'm becoming wanton with need.

"You're going to have to tell me what you want, baby," Oliver says refusing to stop the pleasurable assault he is delivering to my needy asshole.

"Fuck me, fuck me with your cock." I beg.

Oliver smiles down at me and says, "As you wish, my love." He pulls off his pants and rubs some lube on my gaping hole. He brings his hard cock to my entrance and slowly inserts it. He pulls it out and I groan aloud. Oliver laughs and then inserts himself inside me in one motion. He stills for a second as I adjust to the size, having not had him inside me for a few days.

"Mmmmmm, Raven, you're so tight." Oliver moans and begins grinding against my ass.

"Fuck me hard," I demand and Oliver begins thrusting into me; slowly at first, his balls slapping against my ass as with every hard and decisive thrust. But then he picks up the pace as he begins slamming into me. I moan loudly with each thrust and feel my cock throb in anticipation of my orgasm.

"Harder, " I plead as I become close.

He rocks into me harder and faster and I begin panting as I feel my orgasm building.

"Fuuuuck I'm gonna cum." I say and Oliver grasps my cock as he slams into me and begins jerking me off. Faster and faster as I become closer.

I cum hard and it splatters across my chest, Oliver thrust into me once more and then I feel his warm load begin to fill me. He lays on top of me for a moment and catches his breath before he says, "I love you. And I promise I will trust you from now on."

I pull his face to mine and kiss him deeply before saying, "No matter what happens or what anyone says I give you one hundred percent of my trust. And I know if we stand together we can handle anything that comes at us. I love you, Oliver. I'm drowning in those eyes of yours. I'm falling so deeply in love there is no chance of getting out. And there is no way I'm giving you up to anyone. You are mine." I say emphasizing each last word with a peck on his lips.

He smiles, "Yeah, I'm yours."

CPSIA information can be obtained
at www.ICGtesting.com
Printed in the USA
LVHW091327250421
685473LV00004B/66